Raw Nerves

Saralee Perel

PublishAmerica
Baltimore

First printing

ISBN: 1-4137-3354-9
PUBLISHED BY PUBLISHAMERICA, LLLP
www.publishamerica.com
Baltimore

Printed in the United States of America

Praise for *Raw Nerves*:

"My advice: If you're taking this book to the beach, bring more suntan lotion, because you won't want to leave. It's smart and funny, with characters just quirky enough to ring oh so true and a plot that will keep you turning pages until you've established some serious tan lines."

Alicia Blaisdell-Bannon - *Cape Cod Times*

This book is lovingly dedicated to my husband Bob.

Chapter One

My name is Sophie Green.

I worry a lot.

I am an obsessive compulsive hypochondriac, with occasional bouts of panic attacks and binge eating.

I am also a psychiatrist.

My current list of worries includes, but is not limited to: death, senility, my teeth grinding, and the disconcerting fact that one of my patients has a husband who is very unhappy with me. And I think he's a stalker.

It's not easy being a shrink. Patients often act out their inner desires with their therapist. Usually this means that someone is either in love with me or thinks that I'm like one of their parents. This is called transference.

Every one of my therapist pals has had a patient or two that's scared them. I never did, but now I do. I keep telling myself that dealing with crazy-acting people goes along with the profession in the first place. But believe me, this positive self-talk does not make me feel any better.

My mother always warned me about this kind of thing. Of course, she also warned me about bacterial infections from not changing my toothbrush every month. I'm too old to blame my mother for my bugaboos, but it's just so convenient. "Never say everything's fine!" she'd say. "God will notice and then you're really going to get it."

My poor husband Dan. He hates my job. He always worried that some nut will do something to me. Of course, he's been right to worry.

We have a fifteen-year-old daughter named Robin. She's not like Dan, with his zest for life and his "contentment is the realization of how much you already have" shtick. She doesn't possess my melodramatic sense and my, shall we say, eccentricities.

As a matter of fact, for the past year or so, Robin has been quiet. Too quiet for me. It's probably just normal adolescent development, which is an oxymoron if I ever heard one — you know, like a jumbo shrimp. She's a smart girl, and that's not just a prejudiced mother talking. I often worry that her high IQ causes her problems, since our culture still tells us that "smart girls aren't as much fun." But lately, she's been getting awfully thin. And I seem to be making up for her nutritional deficiencies by going in the opposite direction.

The knock on the door was not doing all that much for my nerves, not that my nerves are intact under normal circumstances, whatever that may be.

"Who's there?" I looked out the peephole, but just saw black.

"Mrs. Green? I have a delivery for Doctor Green."

"I'm Doctor Green. Please leave whatever you have outside the door." I turned my head and yelled to nobody, "Dan, there's a package at the door."

After I heard a van door slide closed, I crept to the peephole again. I never feel sure that the person on the other side couldn't just put his eye to the glass and see me, or rather my eye.

I didn't see anything.

Slowly, I opened the door. There was a bouquet of gorgeous dark red roses on the stoop. I bent down and picked it up. A note fell out. That sweetheart of a husband I've got is always doing marvelous things like this. I wish that I was even half as thoughtful as Dan.

I picked up the note. It was typed. It read, "I could have made the brakes fail."

Jesus.

I saw that the van was now way down the street, but I could still make out that it said Cape Cod Bouquets on the side.

I called information and got their number.

"This is Doctor Sophie Green calling."

"Yes, Doctor Green. Can I help you?"

"A bouquet of roses was just delivered to my house, and I'm wondering if you could tell me who sent it?" Oh, if only it would be this easy.

"One moment please, and I'll see what I can find out. Was there a problem with the delivery?"

"No." I held while he went to check it out.

"I'm sorry, Doctor Green. We received payment for them in cash in an envelope with the order request. I just checked with my partner."

"Didn't you think the note was a little strange?"

"Well, we never saw the note. It came with the order form, and the envelope was already sealed."

"May I speak to your partner please?"

"Of course."

A different voice said, "Was there something wrong with the delivery?"

"No, there was something wrong with the note, and I didn't get your name."

Just because they weren't being helpful was no reason for me to act so surly.

"It's Gerry." I decided to let the last name go. I could always get it another time.

"Gerry," I softened my voice, "when did you receive the note? Was it sent to the store, or just left there?"

"We got it yesterday, in the mail. I threw out the envelope it came in, and I don't remember if there was a return address or not."

I got off the phone with no more useful information than I had before I called. I stuffed the roses in the trash, but I kept the note. Oh man, did this give me the creeps.

It was almost eight, and I had to get ready for work, which included breakfast, of course. Today, I was supposed to begin a weight loss plan. Not that yesterday I wasn't. Now, which diet was it going to be this time? High protein or high carbohydrate? I looked through the kitchen cabinets and decided to test the theory that I could lose twice as much weight if I went heavy on both.

While I was preparing to comfort myself with three eggs, the phone rang.

"Hello, Sophie."

I was scrambling them in real butter. To delay an arterial revolt, the accompanying sausages were made of turkey.

"Hi, Ma."

"I hope I'm not interrupting something important. If I am, you can call me back later when you can find the time."

"Actually..." I held the phone on my shoulder while I scrambled,

"I'm in the middle of making breakfast. How about if I call you in an hour or so?"

"I may not be around then."

The eggs were beginning to lose their bright yellow color. This was not going to be a good day.

"Where are you going?"

"What's the difference where I'm going, as long as it's away from your father?"

The brown crust covering the eggs resembled a street map of New York City. I turned off the burner.

Now, mothers always get a raw deal when it comes to parent blaming, but who else is going to get it? Dads of my generation were generally only weekend parents, and sometimes not even that.

"Mother, please. Could you just tell me what the problem is?"

I hadn't even gotten out of my nightshirt yet. Why don't sons get these kinds of calls? My brother, Mark, got off easy, not that I was the type who would carry on about sibling rivalry until I was eighty-two.

Inhale. Hold to the count of three. Exhale to the count of four.

"I'd really like to hear what's bothering you, Ma," I said. With the receiver tucked under my chin, I went to the bread cabinet.

I heard Dan come in the front door, then head to the closet to hang up his parka.

"Well, Sophie, this you won't believe. Your father wants to throw away money every month on some poor outer world child."

"Third world."

"What?"

"Nothing."

Dan came into the kitchen and mouthed a kiss, which always meant, "Don't tell you mother I'm here. Then she'll want to talk to me."

"Your father says that since he's getting older, he feels that it's his responsibility to give some money back. I told him he never took it from these people in the first place."

"There's nothing wrong with Dad giving to charity."

"You think you know everything. You know what they do with the money? They buy these big radios they carry around on their shoulders. Don't tell me I'm wrong, I've seen it."

I found a puffy dinner roll that went down nicely with a glop of strawberry preserves on top. Heaven, thy name is carbohydrate.

I blew a kiss back to Dan. He went out the kitchen door to the back yard.

"Why don't you try talking it out with Dad?" I said. I'm such an idiot.

Where art thou, oh chocolate?

"You know I can't talk to your father. Don't you want to talk with him like I asked?"

"You didn't ask."

"But that's what I meant."

Ah. The peanut butter jar fell over when I reached for the pumpernickel. It was a sign, or karma, or something.

"Well, if you want my advice, I think you should just forget about it and let him go ahead. And stop making him feel guilty. I can't come up with any other solution." That wasn't what she wanted. I'd never learn.

"You think of me as a typical Jewish mother, Sophie. It's a very nasty term and I don't like it."

"Where did that come from? I never said you were."

"That's how you think of me. I'm just the stereotypic Jewish mother."

Now I'm very sensitive about stereotypes of any sort, but really — my mother was a Yiddisha Archie Bunker. What a combination.

"Well, sometimes you say things that make me feel guilty." I tore a slice of bread in half and alternately dunked it in the jelly, then the peanut butter.

"And you think only Jewish mothers do that? Doesn't Robin say things that make you feel guilty?"

"Of course, but…"

"Let me tell you this. It's not fair to make general statements about a whole group of people. Being Jewish and being a mother doesn't automatically make me a bad person."

"I know that."

"And one more thing," she said. "When Robin says something that makes you feel guilty, guess which side of the family that's from? Dan's Gentile side of course. I know. I've heard her grandmother."

I was glad Dan couldn't hear her.

"I'll call you later," she said. "Your father wants his breakfast."

"Bye, Ma."

I scraped the eggs into the garbage. It was just as well. Somewhere I read that burnt egg white is a carcinogen.

Dan was pacing around the empty February vegetable garden, not to say that it was so full of useful stuff in the summer either.

I waved for him to come in. We sat at the table. I wanted to tell him about the problem that was brewing.

"Have you noticed a dark blue pick-up truck hanging around?" I said.

"No." He looked alarmed. "What's going on?"

"Well, one of my patients is in an abusive relationship, and I think there's a chance that her husband's stalking me — just to scare me, probably."

"Why would he do that?"

"You know about these situations, Dan. He's probably afraid I'll tell her to leave him."

"What are you going to do?"

"I don't know. I'm not even sure her husband is really hassling me. I've seen the truck a few times and I know that's the kind he drives, but then today something really scary happened." I told him about the roses and showed him the note.

He read it, and paused with an incredulous expression on his face. "Sophie, last week you said the brakes were mushy."

"I know, Dan. That's why I'm freaking out."

"Didn't the Chevy people say it was just low on brake fluid?"

"Yes," I said, frustrated. "That's why I'm having a fit. Apparently it wasn't simple like that at all."

"What does this abusive guy do for a living?"

"He's a car mechanic."

"You have to call the police," he said.

"I know."

It was getting very late and I had to get dressed to get to the office on time.

I ran upstairs to dress. The bedroom phone rang.

"Hello?" I said.

"Doctor Green?"

"Yes."

"It's Carl."

"Carl?"

"Elizabeth's husband. You know, your patient Elizabeth Darby?" Talk about coincidental timing. Carl's the guy I just told Dan about. How did this lunatic get my home number?

"She asked me to tell you that she's not going to see you anymore."

"How did you get this number?" I said.

"Elizabeth gave it to me." That had to be a lie. No patient had my home number.

I sat on the bed and took a breath, trying to figure out what the hell to do here. Carl's abusive behavior toward his wife would likely escalate if he had a confrontation with me.

"Let me talk to Elizabeth, please, Carl."

"Sorry. She's not here."

"Where's 'here'? Are you at home?"

"No."

"Well, Carl, it's not my policy to have anybody cancel appointments other than my patients themselves, unless they can't call for themselves. So you'll have to tell Elizabeth that I still expect to see her this week."

"She won't be there."

"I'll call your home and talk to her. Good-bye, Carl."

"She's not there."

Now, I was getting very scared for Elizabeth. I had no choice but to be direct.

"Where is she?"

"Take it easy. She's at her sister's in Quincy."

"Then you better give me the number."

"Can't do that. She doesn't want to talk to you."

"If you don't give me a number where I can reach your wife, I'm going to call the police."

"Wait a minute, for cryin' out loud." I could hear traffic in the background. "I'm just calling to cancel an appointment for her. You don't have to call the damn cops."

"That is exactly what I'm going to do if you don't give me a number where I can reach her right now. Now what is it, or I'm hanging up."

Amazingly enough, he gave me a number. Now I could bring up the note. "What did you mean about making the brakes fail, Carl?"

"What?"

Of course he'd respond as if he didn't know what I was talking about.

"You know what I'm talking about," I said.

"Lady, you're nuts," he said, laughing. "Just like all the shrinks."

He hung up and I dialed Elizabeth's number.

"Hello, this is Doctor Green calling. May I speak with Elizabeth Darby?"

"Hold on, please," said an unfamiliar voice. I could hear whispering.

Elizabeth came on, sounding very tired.

"Doctor Green?"

"Elizabeth, are you hurt?"

"No, I'm fine." I'd heard this lie from her many times.

"Why are you at your sister's?" When someone's in the throes of a violent relationship, I don't waste any time with psychoanalysis.

"I'm um...here because I needed some time on my own. I'm fine though, really. Why are you calling? How did you find out I'm here?"

"Carl gave me your number. He just called me to say you're discontinuing therapy."

"Well, I..." I heard her sigh.

"Elizabeth, please tell me what's happening here."

"We had a fight and I had to get away." I could hear her lighting a cigarette. "I didn't tell him to call you. I just told him that I was canceling this week's appointment because I'd be here." She paused. "I'm really sorry he bothered you. He probably misunderstood me and thought I wanted him to call because I'm out of town."

One of a million rationalizations that didn't add up.

"Elizabeth, is there something you want to tell me? If there's something I should know, I want you to tell me."

"Well, I...um."

I gave her a chance to think, but it was nearly impossible to keep my anxiety out of the picture.

Finally she spoke. "Carl is making it very hard for me to come to therapy. He's always trying to convince me you're giving me the wrong advice. That's what our fight was about."

"Remember our discussion about you not letting yourself get caught up in Carl's ideas?" The way people used the word 'co-dependent', like a lot of fleeting psychology terms, annoyed me. After all, who isn't? But if there was ever a perfect clinical example, it was right here.

"Yes, but it's hard to remember how I see things when he's so convincing."

"I know, Elizabeth. But I know you can. I've heard you stand up for yourself many, many times without folding."

She took a drag from her cigarette. "Yeah, I guess so."

"I have to ask you one more time. Are you hurt?"

An exhale. "No, I'm fine." I'm not sure she knew what those words meant. They were just syllables she said time after time, by rote.

"Will you be in for next week's appointment, then?"

"Yes, I will. I promise."

We hung up and I rushed to get ready for the office. I ran down the stairs to find Dan, who was driving me to work because the other truck was in the shop. With any luck, I'd get there before my ten o'clock appointment.

We drove in our old blue Chevy Blazer. The brakes were working fine. A four-wheel drive truck was a blessing on Cape Cod when the snows kicked in and the plows didn't. Today was one of the Cape's rare winter days when there was sun.

"Did you unplug the coffee pot?" I asked, as we were driving along the winding two lane Old King's Highway, also known as Route 6A. The coastline of Cape Cod Bay was visible between houses.

"Yes, Sophie," he said.

"Are you sure?"

"I'm sure."

I could see expanses of marshland behind the homes. The tall golden grasses of the marsh led to pebbly stretches of sand in front of the ocean. As always, fishing trawlers were anchored in groups way out near the horizon.

After waiting at least twenty seconds, which I could barely manage, I asked, "Do you really remember doing it? I mean, can you picture yourself walking into the kitchen and putting your fingers on the plug and pulling it out of the socket?"

"Sophie," he said, keeping his eyes on the road. "Let it go."

I looked out the window at the old captains' houses, sprawling white estates with additions attached over the course of the past two hundred years. There was nothing more beautiful than these old homes in February, when all the Christmas decorations were gone. They rested soberly, with empty wooden rocking chairs on bare front porches.

I pouted quietly.

"I want to talk about what's going on," he said.

"Me too."

I pulled down the visor and used the mirror on the back to make sure I had nothing between my teeth. For a person of forty-one, I don't look so bad. My features are nothing to drop dead over, just pretty. I don't like my high forehead and my thin hair. Keeping it short and layered makes it look thicker. Aside from a space between my two front teeth, my most distinctive feature is my perfect Elizabeth Taylor nose, for which I thank Liz and Doctor Adelman.

I smoothed out the wrinkles on my good gray pantsuit. Then I picked up the car phone to check in with the answering service.

"Just a delivery person this morning wanting directions to your house," the operator who called herself Number Nine said.

"You mean you gave someone directions to my house?"

"No, I don't know the way to your house. I just gave him your address."

"Number Nine!" I shrieked at her. "You can't give out my home address. Don't you know what I do for a living?"

"I'm terribly sorry, Doctor Green. We get so many calls on Monday mornings and I wasn't thinking. I just looked at the address we use in the computer for billing. I didn't think about it being a problem." I could see Dan shaking his head.

"Look, I have to know this will never happen again. I could be in big trouble because of this."

"I'll tell everyone about it. I really am sorry." She sounded it too.

I pressed the "End Call" button to disconnect.

Dan and I have been married for fifteen years and nine months. We have different ways of looking at things. When the morning paper arrives, he checks the winning lottery number. I check the obituaries. If a travel brochure comes in the mail, he imagines splashing around in a warm sea. I imagine flight wreckage on the beach. Dan's the type of person who says things like, "If you have a problem, do something about it."

He also hums.

Although the name Daniel Green has a Jewish ring to it, he is not one of the Chosen. But that was okay with my folks. I was twenty-six years old already and way past my marriageable prime, in their opinion.

With his blond hair, blue eyes and Nordic appearance, he stands apart from my dark and full-featured forebears. His looks are as sharply contrasted to mine as are our personalities. He is tall and slim and has no weight problem. I'm somewhat short, and do I have a weight problem? Me?

Ha!

"Sophie," he said, breaking through my reverie. "I don't like what's going on."

"Of course not. Who would?"

I had to figure out what to do about Elizabeth. I was debating on discontinuing her therapy. I had to protect myself and my family.

My folks had a tough time with the non-Jewish issue at first, but now my mother thinks of Dan as the best thing since her mother's kreplach, and frankly, so do I, although very few things in life are as good as Grandma's kreplach, especially since they used so much salt in those days.

"Sophie," he said, "I'm worried. And I don't think you're telling me everything."

"Worry and digestive disorders go hand in hand," I said.

"Goddamn it, this isn't a joke." He slammed his hands on the wheel.

"I know how you feel," I said. "Honestly I do. And I don't think of any of it as a joke." I touched his shoulder. "I'm going nuts too."

Normally I loved going to my office on the harbor. For thirteen years, I've been renting the same place in a magical old-but-remodeled tuna fish packing plant. The small gray shingled, weather-worn building has no foundation. It juts out into the harbor and stands on pilings, and therefore shifts and shakes in high winds and storms. Not many other people have offices there, probably because it's so ramshackle. There's just a real estate agent, a lawyer and a guy with a boat rental business who's only there in the summer.

Winter is my favorite time, all gray and white. But it underscores the isolated feeling when no summer tourists are around. Sea ice mounds on the pilings of the adjacent restaurant, closed and boarded up for the season. All the boats moored in the summer are gone other than one lobster boat, called the *Pilgrim*. The captain is the only person I see between appointments when I look out the big bay window in my office. He always has his husky with him. The dog seems to have mastered his sea legs. No matter how rough the waves are when they're heading out to the sea, he keeps his position, like a figurehead, on the flat bow of the boat.

The harbor freezes over many times in January and February. It's called "ice up." The temperature, wind, and cloud cover have to interact in specific ways for the entire harbor to be covered with ice. Somehow, the old captain of the wooden *Pilgrim* seems to know just when to relocate his boat. Whenever he pulls it out of the marina and heads south, there's always a freeze the next day. With changing tides the ice cracks and shifts, making long drawn-out creaking sounds. Eventually the pieces break up and flow away and the lobster boat returns. The captain and I have never met, but he always looks up to see me in the window as his boat passes out to sea.

As Dan and I pulled into the parking lot, a panic attack festered in me. What if Carl came at me with a gun? What if he was there, at my office door now? I could feel the hot body rush that signals escalating anxiety. I kept my chin down to keep my head from shaking and got out of the car.

We went into the building. There was no one there and my anxiety let up.

We began to climb the stairs leading to my office. At the top of the stairs, the door to my waiting room was open. I froze.

Dan saw the open door and ran upstairs ahead of me. "Stay right there," he said.

I could hear him talking to someone. With an approach-avoidance feeling, I went up the stairs and in the door.

Dan was talking to Gracie Brill, my first patient.

"Hello, Doctor Green," Gracie said. "I'm sorry, I guess I'm early."

"How did you get in?" I said.

She looked around, confused. "The door was open."

"Okay, Gracie." I tried to hide my concern. "I'll be a few minutes. Why don't you sit in the waiting room?"

Dan and I went into my office.

"You don't really believe the door was just open, do you?" he said.

"I doubt it but it could have been. You know these locks are pieces of junk. We've come in before and found it open."

I handed him my briefcase so I could take off my coat. He stood in front of me with his hands on my shoulders. "What if something happened to you?" he said. "I couldn't go on if something happened to you." He looked down, but I saw the tears fill his eyes and it broke my heart. "You have to call the police."

"I will, sweetheart. Right now."

I looked at his worried face. Of course he was right. Carl was a time bomb.

I picked up the phone on the desk and asked information for the Barnstable Police non-emergency number. I dialed and it was busy.

"When I leave here, I'm going to buy a decent lock for this door," he said.

"Good." The line was still busy.

Making the decision to call the police actually brought me relief. The same way I feel when I finally make a mammogram appointment I've been putting off for months, even though the next step could be worse than the procrastination.

"Why don't you call the emergency number?" he said.

"I can't. They'd come right over and I don't want the patient you just saw to be in the middle of this."

As he reached in his back pocket for his key, I noticed that he was wearing the new ski sweater I had bought him. It had a band of little deer running around the middle. Then I noticed a mole on his left ear.

"How long have you had that?" I asked.

"Had what?"

"That mole on your ear."

"I've always had it. Please don't get that way you get."

I went to the wooden file cabinet to get Gracie's records. I used my key to unlock it.

"How come I've never noticed it before? How do you know you've always had it?"

"Sophie, please. How does anybody know they've always had something? It's fine. Give it a break." He sighed. "I think you get into these crazy things to change the subject and give yourself something stupid to worry about instead of a real problem."

That couldn't possibly be true.

21

He put my briefcase under the big blond oak desk and looked out the bay window at the sea.

I searched for the third time through the files. I couldn't find Gracie's.

"What's the matter?" Dan knows me so well.

"My patient's file is missing."

In the file cabinet, Brendon, Buchanan, Cromwell. No Brill.

"Dan, you have to go now. I have about two seconds before my session starts."

He kissed me on the forehead, and said, "I'll be working at the center all day, so call me. Okay?"

"You know I will, and Dan…you're wonderful, you know." He left after one more forehead kiss.

Dan's one of the lucky people in life who makes a living doing something he believes will make a difference in the world. He's the director of a youth center in Hyannis. It's in a building that was once used as a Salvation Army shelter. He has two social workers working under him and several volunteers. There are about forty kids who go there after school. Most of them have to go as a requirement from their therapist. They never want to be there at first. Dan is good at getting them to do things that are fun, but in reality are therapeutic. One room is set up like a TV game show and the kids work together as teams to win. Dan has a Ph.D. in psychology but only a few people know that. He doesn't care about being called Doctor.

I called the service again. I keep the ringer off so I'm not disturbed during sessions. Therefore I don't know when calls come in. The operator said that there were three hang-ups within the last ten minutes.

I bet Carl knew I was coming in at this hour and expected me to answer the phone. This was probably connected to Gracie's missing file. But why on God's earth would he want her file? Probably other files were gone, too. I decided to check. Elizabeth Darby's file was also missing.

I tugged at the bottom drawer of the file cabinet. When I got it opened, I reached down for a file. Something squirmy wrapped itself around my finger and I felt a sharp bite.

I jerked my hand back, flinging whatever it was across the room and behind my desk chair. My heart thunked. I was afraid to take a look but I had to know what it was. I walked over and peered behind the chair. It was a sea worm, about six inches long and slimy. It was covered with hundreds of legs from one end to the other. I knew sea worms were used as bait. If you picked one up, it would spin around, wrap itself around your finger and bite.

My heart still pounding, I went back to the file drawer and looked inside. I couldn't really see anything, so I got a ruler out of my desk drawer and gingerly pushed aside a couple of files with it. The bottom of the drawer was covered with a whole mass of the disgusting things, moving. Dozens of sea worms. "Shit!" I jumped back.

Oh, God, please.

I leaned over the chair and got the one on the floor to curl itself around the ruler. I dumped it in the file drawer and slammed it shut.

I closed my eyes and insisted to my brain that it focus on my work. I couldn't wait any longer to see Gracie. I gave myself a talk. I can be a professional in spite of wanting to run out of the building screaming. I knew a surgeon who operated the afternoon his son died. He had to. He was the only one who could do it. And right now, my patient came first.

Gracie Brill, who's thirty-two years old, began therapy two months ago essentially because she wanted to overcome her fear of flying. But only rarely was someone's presenting complaint the real reason that therapy was entered. Usually they needed a symptom as an entry ticket, then we could find out what the real problem was.

Gracie operated a daycare service in her home. She lived alone in a small year-round rental in Yarmouth. Many of her relatives had moved off-Cape and she wanted to be able to fly to visit them. Last week, Gracie reported that she finished her sessions at Cape Cod Airlines New Beginners Flying Club. She should only know that she's seeing a psychiatrist who thinks that the idea of traveling through the sky in a multi-ton machine that has a million vital parts made in somebody's garage by God-knows-who, is an idea that should have gone out with the whalebone corset.

Gracie was single and adept at dating men who were no good for her. Usually she picked the no-commitment distancers or the married ones.

She was lovely, about five and a half feet tall with premature all gray hair that she wore shoulder length and played with frequently.

The gray color was most unusual, but quite flattering. She came to today's session wearing jeans and a big white fisherman's sweater.

"How are you, Doctor Green? Is everything okay?" she asked, as she sat in the brown and white wingback. The other large chair, which I took, was made of brown leather. Each seat was placed on either side of the bay window and they faced slightly away from the view, which could often be too distracting. The angle was such, however, that you could stare out the window at the harbor if you wanted to, which was especially helpful during quiet times.

"Yes, I'm fine," I said.

Gracie was silent for a while. I tried to relax by looking around my office. There was a small blond wooden table in front of the window between the two chairs, which was essentially just for a box of tissues. Other than my desk and a director's chair that I sat in for marriage counseling, there was no other furniture.

In one corner was a hanging brass pendulum that Dan had made for me — kind of a Zen thing, he said. It hangs from the ceiling and nearly touches the floor, where there is a circle of fine white sand three feet in diameter. The pendulum has a pointed end, and with just a feather touch it moves. It begins going back and forth, but slowly changes to oblong circles. Each circle overrides the previous one just a little bit, which makes for beautiful unique designs. I've yet to find a patient who wasn't fascinated and calmed by it. The sea calmed most people too, but you couldn't count on that. Someday it was so rough and swirling that there'd be whitecaps in the harbor.

The tiny office has a wonderfully shabby quality to it, and in a real sense the flavor of a fish packing plant remained. When we'd have a three-day rain storm, I could smell the faint odor of fish. I didn't decorate the walls with diplomas or pictures. Other than a ship's clock above the desk, I kept the walls plain, which was just as well, because when it did rain, drips would snake their way down from the ceiling.

Gracie curled some of her hair around her first finger. Whenever she spoke about her boyfriend she never looked me in the eyes. Finally she turned her head toward the bay window and said, "I wanted to talk some about, you know…Eliot…if it's okay."

"This is your hour, Gracie."

Still twirling her hair, she said, "I know, I know. I just get nervous sometimes." Silence again.

Gracie's boyfriend, so to speak, is Eliot Wohlman. That is, Doctor Eliot Wohlman. He is the chief psychiatrist at the inpatient facility for chronic sexual offenders in Yarmouth. He's also a staff doctor at Hyannis Hospital. He sat next to me at last month's medical staff party. His wife sat next to him.

Eliot had an affair with another patient of mine over five years ago. Her name was Jeanne. She never recovered from the relationship. One night, she took all her mother's Dalmane and never woke up.

Gracie said she had told Eliot she was seeing me and I'm sure that made him uptight. If I ever broke the confidentiality barrier, he'd be out of a job, and probably out of a marriage.

I had pieces of his background in my files because of Jeanne and now Gracie. He was forty-four years old and had one teenage daughter, although as I understood it, not having a son was a vital misfortune for him. His father was a neurologist who didn't think that psychiatry was a respectable medical profession. Eliot received many honors for his work not only with sexual offenders, but with criminals in general, and is considered, at least locally, an expert in his field. I see his name in the paper frequently when there's a story involving psychology and criminal behavior.

I couldn't tell Gracie what I knew about Eliot, of course. She knew that I often ran into him at the hospital, but so far, she didn't push me about what I might know about him. I tried to shelve my thoughts and focus on her immediate concerns.

"I am making progress, Doctor Green." Her finger found her hair again. It might have been my imagination, but I thought I heard my waiting room door open and close. "I won't stand for his sneaking around with me anymore." She looked at me directly. "If he wants to see me, then he'll have to take me places, like normal people do. And I told him just that!"

She believed that progress had been made because she had stood up for herself and asked to be treated in a manner more to her liking. It was hard to keep my opinions to myself, and frequently I didn't, but it was too early in her therapy to be confrontational.

"Good for you, Gracie, for asking for what you deserve," I said. "I hope that you're tremendously proud of yourself."

She blushed and said, "Well, I am."

Gracie's involvement with unattainable men has made for years of unhappiness. She has been unable to have a relationship with unencumbered intimacy, assuming there is such a thing, because she's too afraid of the potential for loss. With the men she chooses, she feels protected from ever facing that possibility. The down side of this is that it doesn't work. Not only does she have an empty space inside and outside, but her attachment to Eliot is just as strong as if he were single. The fact that he is married is only a veil — it doesn't protect her from anything.

"Doctor Green, I also think that it's time that I make a decision about him." She looked at me for an approving nod and got one. "I'm going to talk to him and um…"

I didn't want to push her at such an important junction. It had to come from her.

"I, um…I…" She put her head down and covered her face with her hands. It was hard for me not to step in. "I'm going to ask him. I mean I'm going to tell him that it's either me or his wife." She sat up and looked at me with tear-filled eyes. "I just can't keep going on like this. I'm miserable. I'm so tired of sleeping alone every night and thinking about him and his wife." She took a tissue and wiped her eyes.

"You sound very lonely."

"Oh, I am. I'm lonely, and I'm also disgusted with myself. What kind of a jerk spends her life dating married men?"

"Gracie, you are most certainly not a jerk. You are a very brave young woman who is about to take a courageous step." Although I've heard many patients make the declaration that Gracie made, most do not follow through. But I had hope for Gracie. Like the flying problem, when she made up her mind to do something, she did it.

After talking some more about her courage and commitment, her hour came to a close.

The ship's clock chimed six times, indicating it was eleven o'clock. Gracie, knowing her session was over, stood up. At the door she turned and said, "Good-bye, Doctor Green. It's always so long between appointments."

When I first heard of Doctor Wohlman from my patient Jeanne, the pop psychology topic of the day was women in go-nowhere relationships. Jeanne was crazy about him. I thought at first that therapy wouldn't be too tough, and we would focus on her fears of intimacy and other reasons that she might be attached to a non-committing man. But as time went on, the pathological aspects of her personality and subsequently the inappropriate behavior of Doctor Wohlman took star billing.

They would arrange to meet at out of the way hotels off-Cape, where no one would know him. Jeanne's mother knew nothing of the affair and believed her daughter's phony stories about where she was spending the night. The relationship became an obsession for both of them and Jeanne clung to the belief that Eliot would leave his marriage and be devoted to her someday.

Unfortunately, from social events at the hospital, I also knew his wife. On Cape Cod, as in other small communities, everybody knew everybody, and anonymity was basically impossible. I felt sorry for Nancy, Eliot's wife. She seemed quiet and refined. I avoided her whenever I could. After all, I knew two women involved with her husband.

Gracie possessed the same naive qualities as Jeanne, but Jeanne had a long history of severe depression, which Gracie did not.

Jeanne's suicide still haunts me. A lot. I couldn't shake the guilt. When I was ten years old, my younger brother Jeremy was horsing around near my bedroom window. He accidentally fell out and died. I didn't think he was going to fall. Nobody blamed me. As a matter of fact, my parents went out of their way to try to make me feel that I wasn't responsible. They even sent me to a psychiatrist, which I hated. I suppose my brother's death is correlated with my persistently expecting the worst. And I suppose it has to do with a lot of things, my choice of careers, for example. Sometimes I wonder if every time I help a patient, I subconsciously think I'm paying my dues for what happened.

After Gracie left, I had a little time to look around the building. I was nervous about the door that I had heard open in my waiting room during her session. I decided to deal with the sea worms first. I put on my gloves and gingerly got all of the files out of the drawer. I tried not to look at the squirming mass of worms. I wrestled the whole drawer out and went down the stairs and outside to the dumpster.

In the parking lot, I saw Gracie picking up what appeared to be my files strewn all over the place.

"Gracie," I called and ran to the dumpster. I upended the drawer inside it.

She handed me the stack of files. Hers was on top. She was pale and flustered.

"How did they get out here?" she said.

"I don't know." I couldn't hide how upset I was.

"Don't worry," she said. "I didn't read them or anything." Gracie had never been the type to lie. "But what if somebody read mine?"

I assured her no names were mentioned in her file.

"You're positive? If anybody knew it was Eliot…"

She was protecting him, not herself.

"Yes, I'm sure, Gracie. Try not to worry about this and concentrate more on what we talked about in session. This problem is mine, not yours."

She said good-bye and raced to her car. The packed sand parking lot was surrounded by big blue spruce trees that could have hidden about seven hundred people. Behind the trees were tall sand dunes. Normally that would paint a beautiful picture. But not today. I would rather have seen a Dunkin' Donuts than a sand dune. At least then I'd know there were people around. I leafed through the records. All of them belonged to current patients.

I went back in the building and up to my office. I put the drawer and the files back in the cabinet. The non-emergency line to the police was still busy. I decided to call the emergency line after my last session so no patient would be here to get pulled into the middle of everything.

My afternoon people all had substance abuse problems. One lady drank heavily to quell depression. Another combined alcohol and marijuana to make her anxiety subside, and the third was a binge eater who used massive intakes of food to stuff down her feelings of rage and despair. But then she'd feel even more despair and the only thing that would bring relief was vomiting. In all three cases, the use of the addictive substance made the depression worse.

I started to think about the peanut butter and Ritz crackers in my bottom drawer and with clinical finesse, associated my desire for that magnificent combo with an attempt to take my mind off my fear.

God made it that not only was there Ritz and peanut butter in the bottom drawer, but there was also a phone book. A divine opportunity. I decided it would be smart to find a more specialized office at the police department rather than call the emergency line. I found the Special Services Bureau of the Barnstable Police Department. After a Ritz with a shmear, I picked up the phone.

I gave my name and said, "I'd like to talk to someone about a problem I'm having at my office."

"What sort of problem?"

I don't know why I let this get to me, but I didn't want to have to answer a million questions before being hooked up to the right person. This was hard enough already. Ritz and a dab.

"Please let me talk to a detective. This is a sensitive situation since it involves one of my patients."

A gruff sounding person took over.

"Detective Samms."

I repeated what I had just told the first person.

"Doctor Green, let's meet at your office."

This was so sudden. "You mean right away?"

He laughed. "How about tomorrow at noon?"

I gave him directions and hung up, feeling scared of what would happen after tomorrow's meeting. This was all so new to me. I took a deep breath and looked out at the sea. The sparkles on the surface of the water were hypnotic. But by the time Dan was due to pick me up, the daylight had gone and the sea was black with long fingers of light darting on the surface from street lamps on the other side of the harbor.

I gathered my briefcase and my purse and scooted downstairs to meet Dan in the parking lot. I was excited. I knew he'd be so pleased to hear about tomorrow. I always waited to see the headlights of the Blazer before leaving the building, but calling the police made me feel irrationally safe. So I stepped outside. But Dan wasn't there.

I scurried back up the stairs and checked with my answering service in case he had called to say he would be late. No calls. I tried him at the center and at the house. Then I tried the car phone, which often didn't connect. No luck.

I hate it when this happens. I'm the only one in the building after five o'clock and the harbor is winter-empty. This would be a perfect opportunity for Carl to arrive.

My saner side said that Dan thought I was through at six-thirty rather than five-thirty, since that was frequently the time when I finished. My normal side said that Dan had either been in a car crash, suffered a heart attack, had a ruptured appendix, was beaten up at the center, was rushing Robin to the hospital with internal bleeding, or was lying in the woods in a coma, never to be found again.

Anybody could come up the stairs now, and there wouldn't a single thing I could do about it. The other offices were empty. I was trapped. Trapped in a little room by myself, on a secluded harbor in the winter, without even one damn boater out there.

I locked the door to my waiting room and then went into my main office and locked that door too. If someone tried to break in through the waiting room door, I'd have a few minutes to call the police before they broke into the office.

Who was I kidding? I'd never have enough time. I knew it.

I turned off all the lights so no one would know I was here, and sat looking out the bay window to the street on the other side of the harbor, trying to make out a car the size of the Blazer coming down the road.

As the minutes passed and the night grew darker and quieter, my worry level soared. What would I ever do without Dan? It was an unbearable thought, but one that I often obsessed about at three in the morning.

By this time, I had worked myself into a frenzy, something I was able to do with great ease lately.

Someone rattled the outside door to my waiting room.

Let it be Dan. Please...God. That way I can rip his throat out for being late.

How could I find out who it was without letting anyone know I was in here? Too afraid to open my main office door, I didn't move. The door rattled again. Dan would never do this without calling my name. I knew it was Carl.

More rattling and then a boom, and the noise stopped. Someone was standing in my waiting room, on the other side of my door. I crawled over to the desk and felt for the phone. And then the rattling began on my office door.

I dropped my purse and briefcase, which made a loud noise, and picked up the phone. The rattling stopped.

I heard footsteps go away from me toward the outside door. In one crazy second, I knew that if I didn't open that door right now, I might never know who it was.

I didn't stop to think of being hurt. My instinct was to act.

I flung open the door. Eliot Wohlman was standing in my dark waiting room. I flicked on the light.

"What the hell are you doing here, Eliot?"

He put both of his hands up and said, "Don't shoot."

"That's not funny. What are you doing here?"

"May I at least sit down, Sophie?" Without waiting for my reply, he sat on the couch in the waiting room.

I pleaded silently, "Where on earth is Dan?"

And then I smelled something burning.

I ran to the waiting room door and opened it.

"Don't you smell something burning, Eliot?" I thought it was strange that he stayed on the couch while I ran to the door.

"No, Sophie. I think you've been working too hard. Come sit on the couch with me and take it easy." I continued to stand.

"The reason I'm here," he said, "is because a patient of yours who is an acquaintance of mine told me that someone had gone through your files."

"So that's why you broke down the door?"

"I didn't break down the door. I just gave it a push because it was loose and felt opened."

He sat with his coat on, and his legs extending out in front of him. He looked like a young handsome Eliot Gould, but bigger and taller, which gave him an Eliot-Gould-as-a-lumberjack-in-a-Ralph-Lauren-overcoat quality. Anyone would have thought that this was a perfectly normal scene, with two colleagues chatting at the end of their day.

"What do you want?" I said.

"Sophie. I live a block away. I thought you were here. I just stopped in to see if you had a problem I could help with, and when I opened the door and saw nobody was here, I started to leave."

"But you tried my office door…"

"Of course, I tried your office door." That faint odor of smoke again. Maybe it was just someone's wood fire in the distance.

"Why didn't you just knock?" I asked.

"Because by then I didn't think you were here, but I heard a noise in your office and it looked dark in there, and I thought I'd better check it out. Come on, Sophie. You and I go back a long way. What are you accusing me of anyway?"

I didn't answer.

"What happened to the files?" he said. "Did you find out who took them?"

"I have a detective working on it," I said.

No one was mentioning, of course, the absurdity of me having this conversation with a man who is not only married, but seeing one of my patients, and partly responsible for the suicide of another. Maybe it wasn't Carl who looked through my files. Maybe Eliot wanted to see if he was mentioned in Gracie's records.

"Eliot, I'm fine. You don't need to stay." I looked for telltale signs of anxiety. No redness on his neck. His eyes were steady and focused on mine. His facial muscles were relaxed.

"I just thought you could use my help, Sophie. I'm more familiar with career criminals than you are and I thought..."

"Who said it was a career criminal? We're just talking about someone taking files, aren't we?"

That burning smell again.

He started to leave, now clearly uncomfortable and suddenly in a hurry.

I got to the waiting room doorway before him.

"You sure you don't smell anything?" I asked as he walked around me and began going down the stairs.

He stopped and turned around. "I don't. And I think if you were able to be a little bit objective right now, you'd diagnose yourself as someone who needs to take a break. You're showing all the signs of excessive stress."

"Thanks for your concern."

"I know you don't mean that, and you will probably have a negative reaction to any offer from me to work with your detective. But it is my area of expertise."

He left and slammed the outside door. I ran down the stairs. The smell was getting stronger. Was it an olfactory hallucination? I didn't see anything. I went up and down the first floor hallway, touching office doors, feeling no heat.

Then I noticed a small trail of white smoke coming from under the slatted door of the utility closet.

In a state of panic, I watched as a huge plume of smoke billowed out from the closet, blocking my view of the outside door.

Chapter Two

Monday, 5:50 PM

Even this old building had fire safety requirements. The horrible but welcomed screaming of the smoke alarm brought me out of my standstill terror. I prayed it would send a signal to the fire department.

Deep panting brought the smoke into my chest and I fell while making my way down the hall. Flames were now between me and the outside door. I felt the stairs that would have taken me back to my office, but I didn't think I could make it all the way to the top. I could barely get in a whole breath; the searing pain in my chest was like fire. Quicker and quicker my breathing came, and more bursting pain...causing smaller, faster breaths. The smoke blinded me and I reached out, swinging my arms...frantically trying to find the step again.

What if the alarm doesn't go to the fire department?

Sophie, help yourself, Goddammit.

I can take the pain.

I can.

I found the step and pulled myself up. The smoke thickened as I got to the next step. I coughed a wretched cough, only feeling like I was blowing out the rest of my air. The smoke alarm took on the sound of a huge angry cat, wailing in the night...screaming while he tore apart his prey.

Vinyl covered arms reached under my shoulders.

"It's okay," someone said from behind me.

"Thank you...thank you," I managed to say.

The fireman carried me out of the building. I was hugging him tightly around his neck. Other firemen were running into the building as he took me out into the beautiful air of the cold night. This was the scene that Dan viewed as he pulled into the parking lot.

He raced out of the Blazer and ran to me.

"You can put me down. I'm okay," I told the fireman, who had said his name was Aldrich.

"Dan..." I couldn't stop coughing, but I knew that my body was just trying to get rid of the poisons. When Aldrich put me down I reached out to Dan. "We'll go to the hospital," Dan said. Aldrich, still standing next to me, asked me to sit in the Blazer. In response to his questions, I told him my name and gave him my Marstons Mills address.

"I'm okay. I'm a doctor. I'm just very shaken up." I said, still coughing as he took my vital signs and asked me to stay put.

Dan stayed next to me. "I don't need to go to the hospital, sweetheart."

When Aldrich came back a few minutes later, I had stopped coughing. He took my vitals again, appearing more satisfied than the last time. There was an apprehensive quality to his throat clearing, as he began to say something.

"Do you have any idea how this fire started, Doctor Green?"

"No, I don't." Was he accusing me? "I just know it started in the utility closet." He asked me other questions. "How did it start?" I said.

He shook his head.

"Does that mean you don't know?" I asked.

He shook his head again. "The fire marshal will be in touch with you," he said. Then he suggested we go home, which was just hunky-dory with me. By now, the fire was under control. I couldn't see any damage to the building from the outside. Probably Detective Samms would be the investigator rather than the fire marshal, but what did I know about these things?

On the ride home I told Dan about the sea worms and Eliot's visit. He was appalled by everything. And worried to death, naturally. When we pulled into our driveway, I asked him why he was late.

"I thought you were through at six-thirty," he said.

"I never told you that," I yelled. "I ended at five-thirty." It was so much easier taking my anger out on Dan, rather than on the great unknown.

"Look, Sophie, I'm not the person you should be aiming at right now."

Phooey.

"And you'd better tell me you called the police today, or I'm going inside right now and doing that," he said.

"I did. And that's going to solve everything, right?"

He got out of the car and slammed the door. What the hell was I doing? I opened my door and yelled out, "Hey, you want to play fireman and burn victim?"

"You are not funny."

"Look!" I called as he strode to the front door. "I'm trying to make things tolerable, okay? A little joking wouldn't kill you."

"I'm not in the mood," he said and went inside.

I called for Robin the second I was in the door. Every action had such an urgency to it lately. She sauntered down the stairs.

"You don't look so hot, Mom."

"I'm fine. Just hungry."

"Well, that's something new."

I remember the days when I would make a sarcastic comment like that to my mother and it would send her to bed for the rest of the afternoon.

I was so glad to be home. My wonderful home, so warm, so lovely, so safe. I went upstairs and changed into my nightshirt.

Our tiny gray-shingled cottage looks straight out of a Best of New England catalogue. Well, best of Cape Cod garage sales catalogue. In front of a wood stove in the living room, we have a round multi-colored braided rug. One day I counted twenty-three colors.

There's a big copper wash basin, a flea market find, that we use to hold wood next to the stove. Dan thinks we share the chore of wood toting from the pile out back because I lie about doing it.

The couch, in front of the windows, has sink-into beige flowered cushions. On either side are very old stately mission oak chairs in which no one ever sits. We have four pillows, large enough for lolling, in front of the stove. And that's really the best place to sit.

I went into our kitchen, my cocoon of late. I sat down at the old round oak table that was my grandmother's. It bows a little in the middle from heavy fruit bowls she'd always keep full.

I made Dan promise not to tell Robin what happened. I decided to use my family as a drug, hoping to find an altered state in which I could escape the terror outside. I got up and spent about an hour putting dinner together, loving the predictable routine of it all.

Robin had condescended to join us and gifted us with her sparkling conversation.

"I'm sick to death of this meal," she said. Robin is a beautiful girl. Her long straight brown hair was always so perfectly parted on the side. She was tall and thin like Dan, but had bold features like mine. Robin shared my distinction of having a space between her two front teeth. Oddly, we both liked this feature. We used to love having water-spitting contests through our spaces, but she grew out of that.

I had to put my fear out of my mind for this short time. If I didn't, I'd fall apart.

Tonight's meal was one of my standards. It was our low cholesterol, salt-free, low fat, high fiber, no sugar, chicken without the skin, salad without the mayonnaise, zucchini without the butter, meal. The fact that it was healthy made this one of my favorite meals. That's because it made it easy to rationalize my ten PM bowl of Heath Bar Crunch ice cream. The five after ten decision of putting the peanut butter chips on top was another story.

A person could go crazy if they didn't eat under stress.

"Thank you, Robin, for sharing your feelings with us tonight," I said in my sensitivity group leader tone. She hated that. She got up and turned on the countertop television to a loud game show. I hated that. My expertise as a parent kept me in absolute awe.

"Robin," I said, as I noticed her taking only mini-bites of lettuce. "I'm worried that you're not eating enough."

"I'm fine."

"But sweetheart, your jeans are falling off of you. Are you trying to lose weight?"

She looked at me and rolled her eyes. "You want me to be fat, Mom?"

I tried to contain myself. I picked up my fork and continued eating. "No, of course not. But you're anything but fat."

"That's what you think. You're my mother."

"Robin, you hardly eat a thing lately."

She pointed to her plate. "I eat plenty. See?" On her plate was just lettuce. She got up to empty it into the trash can. I was pretty sure that hidden underneath the lettuce was the chicken that she hadn't touched.

After dinner, Dan went upstairs to take a shower and Robin went to her room. I checked the dead bolt on the front door three times before flopping down on the pillows in front of the wood stove. Then came a knock.

I didn't move, but it was obvious we were home.

Another knock. Shit.

I got up and crept to the peephole and saw Eliot Wohlman's face on the other side.

"Eliot, what on earth are you doing here?" I let him in.

"I tried calling, but your line's been disconnected."

"What? That's not true."

I picked up the phone next to the couch. There was no dial tone.

"I'll be right back," I said. "I want to get Dan."

He grabbed my arm. "I can't stay." He didn't let go.

"Eliot!"

"I'm leaving, Sophie. I just came by to see if you were all right. I heard about the fire on the scanner. But obviously you're fine and you don't want me around."

"Don't go yet." I wanted to figure out why all of a sudden he's gotten so worried about me seeing Gracie. Perhaps some community gossip was bubbling. Maybe if I got him talking, I'd hear some clues. "I suppose you called the police after you heard about it on the scanner?"

"Of course I did. Don't be surprised. They discuss their cases with me all the time."

"Eliot, why are you getting so involved with me lately?"

"To help you. Why do you think? I've never known you to be paranoid."

"I'm not paranoid," I said. "But we were never such good buddies before today."

"What is it about me that gets to you so much, Sophie?"

I wanted to tell him that I thought he was a vile person for screwing up so many lives.

"You don't get to me, Eliot."

"I know I do. You've never forgiven me for what happened to Jeanne." That was the first time he had talked about her to me. "But I think the person you really can't forgive is yourself."

Unfortunately he was right, but I didn't want to hear it from him.

"That psychiatrist crap doesn't work with me, Eliot."

"It's better to bring it all up and face it," he said.

Now I was getting steamed. "You don't know what you're talking about," I said.

"Anyone could have made the same mistakes you did. Anyone could have missed the signs." He put his arm on my shoulder. I shooed him off. "I knew Jeanne well," he said. "It was partially my fault too."

No shit.

"I thought there was a possibility of her killing herself, Sophie. I should have told you that."

I hadn't planned on giving him my opinion on his lethal womanizing, but I was getting close.

"Okay, Eliot. I'm not going to talk about Jeanne with you. But now that you've come to my home and you've seen that I didn't get destroyed in the fire, don't you want to tell me what the police said?"

"In spite of everything, I really do want to help you," he said, "but it will take you a while to understand that, judging from the tone of your voice."

"Well, you haven't helped yet. What exactly did the police say?"

"They don't know who put that hot plate there, Sophie."

I hid my shock.

"Well, I'm sure they can find out," I said. "How did you know about the hot plate?"

"You know I've worked with the police for years. They trust me."

"Then perhaps you can tell me. How did the hot plate start the fire?"

"You don't know about any of this, do you?" he said.

"I have my ideas."

"Then I bet one of your ideas is that the hot plate had paper towels on it, and it was attached to a timer set to go off at five-thirty. Was that one of your ideas?"

The sarcastic shmuck.

"Do you have anything more you want to say to me, Eliot?"

"I'm leaving," he said abruptly. "You're not open to talking with me and you don't want me here."

"That is correct," I said.

He turned around and left. I slammed the door behind him. I

leaned against the locked door for a minute. Then I remembered the phone. Instead of asking Dan to solve this one, I decided to tackle what I could by myself. After I heard Eliot's car pull away I went outside to the truck and brought in our cell phone. I called our home number and heard a voice saying that it was disconnected and no further information was available. I wondered if Eliot somehow had it disconnected so that he'd have an excuse to come to my home. But why now? I've known about his affairs for years. I called the phone company and got a recording stating it was after business hours but that there was an emergency number available. Any alternative to passivity was good for me, so dropping my "I hate to bother you" attitude, I dialed the number.

The woman told me that someone had obviously called to request a disconnection.

"But this is my home number. No one from here called you."

"Someone must have."

"Can anybody just call up and ask to have a phone number disconnected without proving who they are?"

"We don't ask for proof. People don't generally call to have someone else's line disconnected. That would be a dirty trick, wouldn't it?"

"That's an understatement. I'd really like my phone hooked back up right away."

"That won't be a problem. I'll put in a work order and first thing in the morning you should have your phone back."

"Thanks. One more thing?"

"Yes?"

"Is there any way of finding out who ordered it to be disconnected?"

"I already checked that order while we were talking and all indications are that you called in yourself to have it done."

Chapter Three

I ran upstairs to tell Dan what had happened. The television was on in the bedroom. He was propped up on the bed pillows, but his eyes were closed. I hated to wake him but I knew I'd never sleep. I turned off the TV and covered him up. Then I quietly picked up my green velvet jewelry box and went to Robin's room, looking for the warmth I desperately needed to be there.

I knocked on her door and she said to come in. My agitation was apparently evident.

"What's the matter, Mom?"

I didn't want to tell her about the phone. By the morning it would be back on anyway.

"I've had a tough day, sweets."

"What happened?"

"Nothing unusual, just a patient who's acting up. This kind of stuff happens all the time."

I had learned years ago how to hypnotize myself at the end of the day so that I didn't obsess on my patients' problems all the time I was home. Every therapist had to learn to do this or we'd all go crazy. Of course this was getting harder and harder to do lately. With enormous concentration, I put the phone and the rest of it out of my mind and focused on my daughter.

"What are you up to?"

"Nothing."

She was so hard to reach. It's a wonder that I do so well with my adolescent patients.

I sat on her bed and looked at her. In spite of her moodiness, my daughter was my saving grace. I felt such love for her it hurt. She was facing away from me at her vanity, wearing a yellow nightgown. I

41

started rummaging through my jewelry box. She turned around.

"I knew that sound would get your attention," I said.

She rolled her eyes.

"Remember when you were little, whenever you'd get sick you'd sit on my bed and go through my jewelry box?"

"That was a long time ago, Mom."

"Robin, I know it's uncomfortable for girls to talk to their mothers about anything important." At least she was still facing my direction. "Come sit next to me." I patted the bed and she came with only the slightest obligatory reluctance. I put the jewelry box between us — not to bribe her, although I'd stoop that low in a second if I thought it would work — but to distract her so she could talk without feeling I was too close. She daintily fingered some of my necklaces.

She pulled out a leather necklace with a big wooden peace sign dangling from it. "You didn't wear this, Mom."

"I did. About a hundred years ago."

She continued to root around the box.

"I worry sometimes that you may be unhappy," I said.

Without taking her eyes from the jewelry, she said, "Well sometimes I am."

"Do you think you can tell me just a little about what's going on?"

"Um…I don't have any friends, Mom. Nobody talks to me."

"Well that must feel terrible," I said.

"It does."

"Do you know why nobody talks to you?"

"I have some ideas." She picked up a pink seed pearl bracelet and held it up to the light. "They think I'm too smart. And I never know what to say to anybody, so people think I'm a snob."

I wanted so badly to solve her problems.

"Don't tell me it doesn't matter what people think, Mom, because it does, and I'm really sick of this whole thing."

"I didn't realize that things were so bad. Is this why you're not eating much anymore?"

"Mother — why do you keep bringing that up? I eat enough. That has nothing to do with what I'm talking about."

She put the seed pearl bracelet around her wrist. She looked at it a minute, then carefully put it back in the box.

"You know if people ever got a chance to know you, they'd really like you."

"You're my mother. Of course you'd think that."

"How bad does it get?" I said softly.

"Don't be dramatic, Mom. I haven't slit my wrists yet."

I knew her sarcasm meant that our moment was over.

I picked up the seed pearl bracelet. "This looked good on you." I put it around her wrist and clasped it. "My parents gave this to me when I graduated from medical school, and now it's yours."

She looked me in the eyes. "Thanks Mom. Are you sure?"

I reached to hug her but she got up quickly and looked at the reflection in the mirror of the bracelet on her wrist. She was back to her distant mode. And I always took that so personally.

I watched her put a yellow barrette in her hair and take it out. I could watch her for an eternity. My little girl. So beautiful. I couldn't find the right words to say to her. I got up to leave. "Sleep well, Robin."

I went to our bedroom. Dan was sound asleep, facing away from my side of the bed. I felt very lonely. Under the covers, I faced away from him, but I wedged my feet between his knees for warmth.

By the time morning came, I had slept only two or three hours. I heard Dan fling himself out of bed and go downstairs. I picked up the phone next to the bed. It was working.

Dan tended to bounce in the morning. I tended to trudge.

Unlike me, he drank decaf. He liked the taste of it and didn't need the lift of the real stuff. I couldn't care less about the taste, and would be just as happy getting the caffeine intravenously. He also liked non-alcoholic beer. Go figure.

When I went downstairs, he was already in the backyard at his therapeutic hideaway, the compost pile. Robin was looking through the fridge. Then she looked through the cabinet, found a can of cashews, opened it and ate one. Last night's talk was a treasure for me, but by now was in the far reaches of my daughter's mind, where it would stay for a very long time.

"Mom," she said, on her way out of the kitchen. "I was thinking of staying late after school today. There's a girl who needs help in math and she asked me to meet her and help her. Do you think I should?"

Funny how dependent kids could become as they began emancipating. She didn't need me to tell her if this was a good decision. She knew it was. But I didn't want my daughter to drive a car until she turned thirty-five, much less stay late at school. Not with everything going on. But what was I going to do? I couldn't keep her locked up until all my problems were solved.

After thinking for a minute, I decided to be the perfect mother. I said, "I have faith that you're smart enough to make your own decision here." She needed to hear that, I knew.

Of course, it was a lie. No mother has any faith whatsoever in her fifteen-year-old child, but we've all read the same parenting books about letting the arrow shoot from the bow or something nobody wants to hear like that.

She turned and left the kitchen, the cashew evidently qualifying for her nutritional breakfast needs. I worried about her food issues. And yet, I knew from experience that focusing on it too much could make a problem develop that wouldn't necessarily have blown up to problem strength. She was skinny, but not remarkably so. On the other hand, how could I let my daughter possibly become a full-fledged anorexic and not do anything to help her?

"Thanks, Mom."

Dan returned from the compost pile. He wanted to share with me a most fascinating story about the relative stages of decomposition of tomatoes versus egg shells. I didn't want to change the subject but I needed to tell him about the phone and Eliot.

I think men can generally take a break from anxious preoccupation better than women can. He took a Diet Coke can out of the trash and put it in the lovely bucket full of recycled cans we keep next to the sink. Ah Dan, the preservationist — always trying to save something — the earth's resources, the Cape's dwindling undeveloped space, his troubled kids at the center. I agree with the idea of recycling of course, but I only do it if I think somebody's watching.

How hard it must be for my husband to be able to help save everything he cares about except his wife.

"Sit with me, Dan." I said. He took the chair next to mine. I reached for his hand. He held mine tightly. I took a deep breath and then told him that the phone had been disconnected.

Before giving me a chance to continue, he rushed to the wall phone and picked it up. "It's working, now," I said. "I called the phone company last night. But there's more." And I filled him in on Eliot's visit. Like most people in our line of work, Dan had heard about him.

I could see the wheels turning in his brain, trying to sort everything out. "I'm going to be fine, you know. We'll solve this problem. Once I tell the detective about Carl, he'll be able to arrest him."

Sweet Dan, his face so full of anguish. "It won't be that easy, Soph. You don't have any proof it's Carl. It could be Eliot."

"But the business with the brakes..."

He shook his head. We were both so frustrated.

"I know Carl's dangerous," I said. "And the police will pick him up, won't they? I mean, I certainly have just cause to suspect him."

I started to cry. He tenderly brushed a tear from my cheek. "I know our profession carries these risks," he said. "But this whole thing has been just too much. What if they arrest Carl and things keep happening?" he said.

"You always tell me not to worry about anything until it happens. Can't we just wait and see if the detective can piece it all together when I tell him about all that's been going on?"

He kissed me softly, then put his arms around me. "We'll have to wait. But I'm not good at that. I just wish I could make it all better."

I held him. "Oh — you manly man." He laughed. Then I laughed too — a cleansing moment. "This will be behind us soon. I know it will," I said.

The telephone rang.

"Hello?"

"Sophie, thank God you're there." It was Ruth, my eighty-year-old neighbor. We rarely see our neighbors. Everyone keeps to themselves other than when there's a power outage or something and we all want to help each other.

"What's the matter?" I said.

"Have you been outside?"

"No, but Dan's been out back. What is the problem? You're making me very nervous." I could see Dan's face flush.

"You better go out front," she said.

"Just tell me!"

"Oh Sophie, there's a big swastika on the front of your house!"

"On the front of the house?" I screamed.

"Yes." Her voice was trembling.

I flung down the phone and ran out front with Dan. It was spray-painted in black and it had to be at least five feet wide. It was poorly drawn, but it was unmistakably a swastika.

Ruth and her husband came out from their house. Robin came running from the front door.

"Mom. Who would do this?"

"I don't know." I felt disgust. "We have to call the police," I said.

Ruth and her husband were standing in their bathrobes. I expected to see indignation on their faces. Instead I saw fear.

"Ruth," I said, "this is from one of my patients. You need to know that this is against me. It's not against you or anybody else in this neighborhood." She had a faraway look in her eyes. "I promise, Ruth. It's just against me."

Her husband put his arm around her and slowly led her back to their home.

I called the police who arrived in less than five minutes. A reporter and a photographer from the Hyannis Sun Times arrived too.

"Do you have any idea who did this?" the reporter asked Dan, after writing down our names. I motioned for him to say, "No."

"What do you do for a living, Mr. Green?"

"Don't, Dan. Don't answer," I said. "I'm sorry to be so evasive," I said to the reporter. "I don't want the place my husband works printed in your report. It would probably be the next target."

"Your occupation, Mrs. Green?"

"I'm a psychiatrist."

"Do you suspect that one of your patients has done this?"

"The average person who sees a psychiatrist isn't necessarily crazy," I said. Thank God I had the meeting scheduled with Detective Samms. I didn't want to screw everything up by saying things I shouldn't right now.

The photographer snapped pictures of us talking. The swastika was in the background. One of the policemen interrupted the reporter and called us aside to ask questions.

"Wasn't it your building that had the fire last night?"

I was so glad the reporter couldn't hear this.

"Yes, officer. I'm having some difficulties with somebody at the office. I've been getting other threats. I have a meeting with Detective Samms in a few hours."

"Well, I'll give him this report then." He had some sort of solvent with him. He gave it to Dan who went over to the swastika. He tried to clean off the paint. When he was through, I could still see a faint outline of it on the shingles.

By the time everyone had left, I was enraged. I got dressed for work as quickly as I could and then I grabbed the truck keys.

"I'll be back in an hour, Dan."

"Where the hell are you going?" He tried to grab the keys.

"I'll be fine. I'll be back before you know it." I didn't want him to know where I was going and try to talk me out of it.

I climbed in the Blazer and quickly pulled out of the driveway. Eliot Wohlman was going to pay for this for the rest of his life. I knew he was Jewish and would know how much a swastika would sting.

It took me only ten minutes to get to his clinic in Yarmouth. It looked more like a prison. I had never been there before, and was frightened going in.

The building was red brick and was situated between two large warehouses. With difficulty, I pulled open the massive front door. Directly inside was a glass-enclosed booth with a receptionist at a desk.

She leaned toward the small slotted opening in the glass and said, "Yes?"

"I'm here to see Doctor Wohlman."

"Do you have an appointment?"

"Yes," I lied.

I waited while she called Eliot. After she hung up, she pointed toward a door on the left and pressed something so it would unlock.

"He said you know the way."

I went through the door cursing Eliot to myself because he knew I didn't know where to go.

I went down a long hallway, with dirty tiled floors and concrete walls. I passed a room where I heard a bunch of people yelling. Quickening my steps, I came to the end of the hallway where there were two more doors. I opened the one on the right and saw what looked like a large waiting area with benches against the walls. There were four men sitting there, all wearing blue overalls. They each looked at me.

"Excuse me," I said, wanting to get the hell out of there. "I'm looking for Doctor Wohlman's office."

One man stood up and came towards me. He took out a cigarette and lit it slowly. The others made it obvious they heard me, but that they weren't going to help me. Sexual offenders had no status in the community, naturally, but they sure seemed to think they could make up for it in here.

"I'll take you there," the man near me said. When I looked closely, I saw that he was only about eighteen.

He led me through another door. Inside was a long stretch of offices. We walked about twenty feet and came to an office with Eliot's name on the door. I thanked him and he walked away.

It was then I removed myself from my fear and remembered why I was there. I did not knock.

Eliot was sitting behind his big desk, reading a newspaper. "I didn't know we had an appointment, Sophie."

He put down the paper and asked me to sit. I didn't.

"Do you like scaring old people?"

"What? Sophie, please sit down."

"What is it you've got against me all of a sudden, Eliot?" I remained standing. "The swastika came off. But I can still see it there. And every time I see the outline of it, I'm going to remember what you've done and what type of a person you are."

"You're crazy," he said.

"You're absolutely right. I'll never forget that you did this, Eliot. And you're going to pay for it in ways you can't begin to imagine." I wanted to make him nervous.

"What are you talking about?" He knew I had the power to screw up his marriage. He just didn't know if I would use it.

I turned and left his office and the building.

When I got home, Dan was immensely relieved to see me. I told him where I had been. "I'm going to drop you off at work," he said. "Then I'll be at the center. I'll leave from there ten minutes before noon so I can meet you and Samms."

It was a drive filled with tension and fear. I prayed the detective could help us solve this problem right away, but I knew I was probably being naive. And now, I couldn't decide if it was Carl or Eliot behind the threats.

When we got to my building, everything looked oddly business-as-usual. One would never have known there was a fire here last night. Only the paint in the hallway needed redoing. It gave a false sense of normalcy. Dan walked me to my office then we said goodbye. I checked myself out in the waiting room mirror to make sure I wasn't too disheveled from the rush. I was wearing my winter black, a long skirt with a cowl neck sweater. I have lots of summer black too.

An icy rain began to fall. I hoped it might wash off the last trace of the swastika, but if the solvent didn't do that, the rain probably wouldn't either. I tried to center myself by looking at the sea. It appeared so tranquil. Gray like the sky, almost blending with the horizon. I looked down from my window and watched the pattern of the drizzle dappling the surface of the water. Then my breathing slowed to almost normal.

My first appointment was with Carl's wife, Elizabeth Darby. I would have to tell her that I believed I was in danger from her husband and I would be bringing in the police. I knew she'd be hysterical hearing this. But if I didn't do something to protect myself, I'd be behaving in the same passive pathological manner that she's been doing all along.

Elizabeth was a forty-two-year-old survivor of childhood sexual abuse. This was her third marriage to an abusive man.

When I first met her, about a year ago, she said matter of factly, "I was sexually abused by my father from age eight to twelve. He had sex with me nearly every night except Friday and Saturday, when he was too drunk to stand up. Those nights he usually beat up my mother. I know I'm supposed to be honest with you, so I wanted to get this out in the open right away." I was dumbfounded to hear this information during a first session and equally surprised at her unemotional attitude.

"Have you read many books about sexual abuse?" I said.

"I've read all the bestsellers. I don't hate my father. In fact, I love him."

"Why have you come to therapy?" I asked.

"Because my husband thinks I'm frigid and because we argue a lot. He thinks I need to get my head on straight."

"But why do you want therapy?"

"I just told you."

"No, you told me what your husband wants, not what you want."

"Well…" She paused, and turned to look at the sea. "I'm not sure."

Elizabeth was a good-looking woman, with long red hair and a face covered with freckles. Her large glasses had a light green tint that accentuated her green eyes. She often dressed in a flashy manner and during her first session was wearing an orange sweater with tight white velvet pants and black cowboy boots. In spite of the aggressive-looking style, her inner nature of obedience showed through. So much came out in this first session. She was desperate for help.

"I guess I've been pretty unhappy and when Carl, that's my husband, told me I better get myself together, I just figured he was right."

"Why have you been unhappy?"

"Well..." She took off her glasses and rubbed her eyes. "My marriage stinks, frankly. I never feel like...well, you know. I...um...never feel like having sex." She put her glasses back on. "I'm so tired and I feel so ugly and all."

"What makes you think you're ugly?"

"Well, not ugly, I didn't mean that, just not pretty, you know...just not looking good...or feeling good for that matter."

"Tell me a little about Carl."

"Well, he's a car mechanic, first of all."

"And what is he like?"

She was quiet for a moment. "He means well. It's just that sometimes he doesn't understand me. When I'm feeling bad, he takes it personally, like I'm feeling rotten to get back at him for something. He thinks I don't want to have sex because I hate him. He thinks if I loved him I'd be turned on, not all the time of course, he's not that weird, but more often than I am. We've only been married three years, Doctor Green."

"What do you think of Carl?"

"I don't know." She thought for a minute. "He adores me."

"But, he doesn't like some of your...moods?"

"No, he doesn't."

"And you feel that if you can just get rid of these moods and become more sexually aroused, then you'd be a great wife?"

"Yes, exactly, exactly!"

I remember pausing then, and looking out the window at the ocean. So calm amidst the angst I was witnessing.

"Why do you think you have these moods, Elizabeth?"

She took off her glasses again and rubbed the bridge of her nose.

"I don't know," she said. "Maybe it's hormones. I am forty-two and maybe I'm going through the change early?" She looked at me with hope in her eyes.

"Have your periods been less regular?"

"No, not yet."

Then we both looked out the bay window. The ice was beginning its winter thickening on the pilings.

"It would be nice, Elizabeth, if we could determine that this was all a hormone imbalance and not a marital problem, wouldn't it?"

She put her glasses back on and looked at me. "I guess you don't believe that."

"No," I said. "I don't."

And today, a year later, Elizabeth is about to hear some bad news from me. But I had to time it right — although that didn't seem possible.

Now the cold rain came down in heavy waves. Elizabeth kept her red coat on as she slowly sat down in the wingback. The wind howled and swirled around the building. With each loud gust, the room moved slightly and the clock swayed. It must have been dead low tide, when the pilings didn't have enough support from the surrounding water to stay still.

"It's freezing in here, Doctor Green." She pulled her collar up around her neck. I got up and turned on the space heater I bought from Sears. Though I paid through the nose for utilities, the heat barely reached the second floor.

"Thanks," she said. She removed her glasses and rubbed her forehead. I saw what I thought was a bruise on the bridge of her nose that was covered with make-up. I knew a part of her wanted me to see it, or she wouldn't have taken off her glasses. A cry for help that was equal in intensity to a desire to stay the same.

"God," she said, "am I glad to be here. I felt terrible when you called me in Quincy. I made such a mess of things."

"Think about it first, Elizabeth. Think about the reality before you accuse yourself."

She raised both hands in a familiar way and nodded repeatedly as if to say, I've heard it all before but I'm not convinced.

"I know what you're trying to say," she said, "but the truth is if I could only learn what upsets him so much, then I could avoid making him so upset."

"So it's your responsibility that he hits you?"

"Well, when you think about it...yes. If I said or did something different, he'd act differently."

"Elizabeth, let me say it straight. Carl hits you because he can't control his aggressive impulses."

"But if I..."

"You could try to second guess what will set him off until you're blue in the face, but you'll never win at the game."

"Why do you say that?"

"Because anything can set him off! His violence is not logical. You can say something one day and it would be fine, and the next day it would turn him into a lunatic. This is his problem with anger, control and aggression. It's only your problem because you stand for it, and...you take the responsibility for it."

"Don't hate me for saying this. I'm not really defending him. I'm not. But Carl's had a really difficult life. He's had a lot of awful things happen to him."

A group of seagulls flew slowly right outside the bay window. They broke our concentration for a second. One was having a tough time moving forward against the wind. We watched as he struggled and then with great effort caught up to the others.

"I know you have compassion for Carl," I said, "but it doesn't excuse his behavior. No one should tolerate abuse of any sort, Elizabeth. You should be furious at Carl. If you think that you can dance around him for the rest of your life and just be a good little girl regardless of what he says or does, then you're asking for very sore feet and lots of foot baths with boric acid, because no matter how long or how far you dance, you'll always be facing the same lousy dancing partner." Elizabeth laughed at the analogy. She stayed quiet for a moment and so did I.

"I felt the same way with my dad, you know."

"I know."

"I thought that I had to have done something wrong or he wouldn't have punished me so much." She used the term punished in place of the words "sexually abused."

"Your father would have punished his little girl even if she was the epitome of perfection. It had nothing to do with you, Elizabeth."

"But how do you know that? How do you really know that?"

"Let me put it this way. Does any little girl deserve to be punished the way you were?"

I remained silent and let her think.

"No. No matter how bad the kid is, she doesn't deserve to be punished that way," she said.

She had about a million miles to go. Elizabeth married Carl so that she could repeat her past in an effort to correct it. If Carl would stop abusing her, it would feel, psychologically, as if her father stopped. But she was stuck in this bind. Because, by definition of the original problem, she had to marry an abuser and Carl was not going to change.

I looked across the harbor and saw the *Pilgrim* swaying with the roiling waves.

"I need to tell you what happened last week," she said. "I'm not trying to change the subject. It's just that it's important."

"I'd like to hear about it."

"Okay." She took a deep breath. "Here's what happened," she began. "We were both sitting on the couch watching TV. Carl began telling me about a fight he had the day before with some guy who thought he charged too much to fix his car, and then didn't think he fixed it the right way to begin with."

She stopped talking abruptly, feeling every account was a betrayal. A noisy gust made the building shake. She didn't notice. A low squeaking sound came from the pilings beneath us that held up the building. I always worried I'd hear one crack.

"Okay," I said. "Go on. It's okay to tell me about it."

"Well, he nearly killed the guy. They took him away in an ambulance! Carl had him on the floor and he tried to shove him under a car that was on a lift, and he slammed into the car so it would fall on the guy! People pulled him away, but he had already broken the guy's jaw."

"How did this all result in you going to your sister's?"

"I made the mistake of telling him that I thought what he did was wrong. I even said it in a normal tone of voice. I didn't yell at him or anything. And I didn't call him names, or do anything that I thought would set him off. But something I did obviously set him off, because he started smacking me. He just kept punching me. I tried to get away, but he kept pulling me back and hit me some more."

"Is that what that bruise is from?"

Embarrassed, she looked away.

"The whole situation got worse. He got one of your cards out of my purse and dialed your number. I tried to yank the phone out of his hand but I couldn't. He slammed down the phone after he got your service. Then he dialed your home phone and I pushed the button down so it didn't go through."

"Do you know how he got my home phone number?"

"He told me he had it a while. He said he called your husband's center during a weekend and got it from someone there. He told whoever answered the phone that he was the father of one of the teenagers who goes there and there was some sort of emergency and he needed to call your husband at home."

"How did he know about my husband's center?"

She looked ashamed. "I must have told him."

"That's okay, Elizabeth. You didn't know what he was going to do."

"Well, after I put my finger on the button, he started screaming at me. He said, 'That piece of shit shrink is behind all this. You never acted this way before you started going to see her.'

"'But Carl,' I said, 'Doctor Green is only trying to help me.'

"He yelled 'Oh really? I think she's just trying to make me mad. She hates all men. That's why she tells you to get the fuck away from me.'

"'But she doesn't tell me that,' I told him. 'She just encourages me to get a life of my own, Carl, and do things for myself sometimes!'" She shivered, more likely from anxiety than the cold. "But there was no reasoning with him, Doctor Green. He ran into the kitchen and got a big butcher knife and he...and he..." She began to cry softly and then she began to sob. I took a few tissues and reached over and put them in her hand. I was hoping she couldn't see my trembling. "He grabbed me, and I turned to run away and he sliced through the air with the knife and took a big chunk out of my thigh." She cried into her hands.

"How horrible, Elizabeth! How did you ever get out of there?"

"I guess I was lucky because he felt bad when he saw all the blood and he put the knife down."

"Did you see a doctor?"

"Well, that afternoon I went to my sister's and when she saw the cut she made me see her doctor. I told her I would only do it if she promised to say that it was an accident and that she had dropped a bunch of stuff where I was standing and the knife hit me."

"And the doctor believed that?"

"I guess so. He just stitched me up and didn't ask any more questions."

So typical of doctors not to get involved with messy abuse cases.

"You're back with Carl now?" I asked.

"Not yet. I spoke with him last night and he was just as angry as he was last week. He knew I had an appointment with you today and that set him off. He even threatened to show up here. He said he'd find me no matter where I tried to hide."

"Elizabeth, it's time to call in the police."

She turned white with fear.

"I can't!"

"You have to protect yourself."

"No! He'll kill me if I call the police."

"Elizabeth, I can't let you leave here and walk right back into a life-threatening situation. I know you don't want to hear this, but I'm going to have to get the police involved." I felt terribly sorry for her. Sometimes it was very hard to be objective and do the right thing.

"It won't do any good," she cried. "If you call the police, it will screw everything up! I can't tell them anything. A restraining order is just a piece of paper. It won't protect me. He'd never stay away! And if I just keep quiet, he'll get to me when they leave." She looked at me intensely and said, "If the police come I'm a dead woman."

She got up from her chair and came over to mine. The rain pounded against the window. The wind was making the building shake and both of us trembled from the movement and our fear. She knelt on the floor and grabbed my hands. "Please! Please! Don't do this. I promise I'll leave him. Just give me a chance to do it."

"Elizabeth, I…"

"I'm begging you. Just give me until tomorrow. When he goes to work, I'll get my things and go to my sister's in Quincy."

Another rise of wind circled the building. Droplets pelted the bay window in staccato. At mid-morning, it was dark. I waited a moment before going on.

"You can't live in fear of him for the rest of your life. We can make this better, Elizabeth. I can get you to a safe place in Hyannis where he'll never find you."

She got off her knees and went back to her chair. She leaned forward and pleaded, "Please don't call the police. I promise I'll get away. I don't want to go to some strange place. I promise I'll go to my sister's. I'll even call you and tell you what happened. I don't want Carl arrested."

"But he abuses you."

"It's my life."

Talk about your basic bottom line.

"I have to do this, Elizabeth."

"It's my life!" she repeated.

"I know that. And I'm going to do what I can to keep you safe. You have to promise me that when you leave here you will go straight to your sister's house." It was time to lay it all out. "I'm talking with someone from the police station this afternoon. I'm going to tell him he can reach you at your sister's."

She sobbed. Tears fell as her shoulders heaved.

"I have to trust you, Elizabeth. I know it's asking a lot for you to trust me, but if you really think about it — in your very soul, you know I am doing the right thing."

The ship's clock chimed six times. She looked pale and shocked. Without saying a word, she put on her coat. "I guess I don't have any choice."

"No," I said softly, "you really don't." And I knew I didn't either.

She left my office. I was worried to death for her.

"Doctor Green!" I heard her shout from the waiting room.

I ran out to find Elizabeth and a man standing in the waiting room. He had a gray crew cut. His hair length matched the stubble on his chin. Only his middle was big, like a beer belly. The rest of him was wiry. He was wet from the rain.

"I'm her husband," he said. Elizabeth looked terrified.

"What are you doing here?" I folded my arms in front of my chest. For some reason I was not afraid.

"I came here to pick up my wife."

There was no reason to have a dialogue with this ape. And that was my first and final judgment. Anybody who doesn't think therapists are opinionated is nuts.

"I'm going back inside," I said. "Elizabeth, do you want to come back into the office with me?"

She took one step forward. Then she took one step back.

"Go ahead, Liz. You're free to go with the doctor."

I beckoned her with my hand. I felt like I was talking someone down from jumping off a thirty-story building.

"Elizabeth, you can come in here with me and then later on you can go home to your husband. You have nothing to lose by coming. I won't do anything. We'll just talk for a few minutes. Mr. Darby can even wait here if he wants. Now, come in Elizabeth. Let's just talk for a little bit."

She broke out of her trance and walked toward me.

Oh, thank you lord.

I turned to go back in my office and she followed.

"Now Liz, hold on." She stopped with one foot inside my office. Then she turned around. "Don't go in there. She's only going to say bad things about me. You know that."

"Elizabeth, why don't you come in here for a second so we can just catch our breath? Then you can leave any time you want." I said. "No one will stop you."

"I'll just talk with Doctor Green for a minute, Carl. Just to tell her everything's all right. Otherwise, she might not think everything's all right...if you know what I mean."

"You take one more step in that doctor's office, and you'll be sorry you did."

"But you just said I was free to go."

"Okay, go ahead. But when you come back out here, you won't find me."

"But, just for a minute...if I don't she'll...Carl, please." Her voice shook.

"You go in there even for one fucking second, and you'll never see me again."

She wavered. I had lost her.

57

She ran to him. He grabbed her arm. "Let's go," he said. They went out the door together, but not before she looked back at me and said, "I'll call you later."

Chapter Four

I stared at the sea. The rain had eased up and now a thick fog was descending. In a few minutes that detective would be here. I knew from experience that Elizabeth could be right about the police. If they went to the house to investigate and everything looked fine, Carl would take it out on her when they left. And she was right about the restraining order. It might just incense Carl, and it wouldn't stop him from coming around. I prayed there was more the police could do. I didn't have a choice here.

Eight chimes meant noon. I opened my door to find Dan and the detective sitting together in my waiting room. I invited them into my office.

Detective Samms looked to be about fifty years old and his tan baggy suit looked to be at least half that. When he took off his coat, I saw a split in the underarm seam. And the coat itself, which was a worn herringbone, had a black stain on the breast pocket somewhat in the shape of a moose. He was on the pudgy side, perhaps five foot ten or eleven, with a sweet face that had small rounded features. He reminded me of the detective in Cagney and Lacey. Most of his black hair was gone and whatever remained curled around his ears. His wrinkle lines indicated that he did a lot of smiling in his life, but he wasn't doing that at the moment.

Dan sat on top of my desk. Samms sat in the leather chair and I was in the wingback, where my patients usually sit. Samms already knew about the hot plate fire, and Dan and I filled him in on the rest. I handed him the note that came with the roses.

"It's one of two people," I said. "You should be investigating Doctor Eliot Wohlman, the director of that clinic in Yarmouth for sexual offenders. He appeared in my office and in my home last night.

He could have set the fire, and I'm sure he was behind the swastika." I didn't mention that his girlfriend, Gracie, was my patient. "He said that he had heard from one of my patients that my files were disturbed."

"Which patient told him that?"

"I can't tell you that."

Samms just shook his head. He might have rolled his eyes too, or maybe I was imagining it.

"He wants to talk with you," I said. "He wants to give you his 'expert' opinion, being that he works so much with criminals."

"I know who he is," Samms said. "In fact he's well respected professionally. Why are you suspicious of him?"

"Too many coincidences," I said. "He showed up the same day that he heard about the files missing, and I didn't like the fact that he was creeping around my dark waiting room or that he came to my house. He probably disconnected my phone too. Maybe he stole the files in the morning to make sure his name wasn't in any of them."

"Why don't you just tell me which patient he's involved with? I'm assuming he doesn't want his wife or the public to find out."

"How on earth did you reach that conclusion?"

"Piece of cake. Why else would he be worried about his name in a file? Unless of course he's doing something illegal. My explanation is the most probable."

I couldn't stand this. Being outsmarted made me edgy. I forced myself to keep a lid on my irritation.

Wallace Samms got on my nerves from the minute we met. I suppose the nature of our relationship is mostly what got to me. I particularly hated being in a situation that I couldn't resolve myself. Plus it was terribly difficult giving out information about my patients. It went against all my ethical codes, but I knew I had to do it. I looked out the window. The fog which usually casts such a beautiful blanket over the Cape was now making me feel smothered. So was Samms. I wasn't trying to be uncooperative but I knew I sounded that way.

I got up and walked to the corner of the office. I pushed the pendulum a little so it began making circles. "There's another person you should investigate. I'm terribly concerned about a violent man and his wife." I told him the whole story, including the danger if the police went to their house. "He's a car mechanic so he would know all about rigging the brakes."

Samms finished writing something on his little notepad. "You did the right thing in telling me about this. Now we can go to the Darby household and get her out of there if she didn't leave for Quincy yet."

"And if she won't go with you?"

"The alternative is doing nothing and hoping that a woman with years of abuse behind her will finally decide to get away, and that she'll be able to make that getaway safely. What are the odds of that?"

I noticed that he often rubbed his left knee. Looked like an arthritic condition. "Okay," I said finally. "We're in agreement with this one."

"This is not a who-can-outsmart-who duel we're having here."

I folded my arms across my chest.

Dan said to Samms., "Could you patrol the office area and our house?"

"I know that would be best," he said. Then he took out a handkerchief from his back pocket and wiped his forehead. The hankie looked to be about as old as the suit. "I'd like to tell you I'll have a man watching you around the clock, but it's impossible. We don't have the resources for that."

He stood up. "We're done for now. I'll check with the phone company about that disconnection order, and I'll look into the bait shops and the florist, but someone would have to be pretty stupid to leave an easy trail. I'm sure there are no useful fingerprints on your file cabinet, but I'll have it checked anyway. You should get a better lock for that thing, or move it. Try to make things a little harder for the criminal."

"I'll get a metal cabinet from Staples." I decided from now on I'd keep all my current files at home.

"Good, although nothing will do the trick if someone wants to get in there badly enough," he said. "Do you have a burglar alarm at your house?"

"No."

"Get one — and make sure it's the kind that connects to the police. I'll arrange for a phone trap on your lines here and at home. If you get a call you want to trace, there's a number you call and they'll be able to trace it. Got that?"

I hated 'got that'.

"I can just press the star button and six nine or something. That will tell me who called."

"No. Callers can block that. We'll have to trap the line. And Doctor Green, I want you to notify me immediately the next time you get a threat of any sort, and I don't want you to touch anything when you see it. Just call me at the station. If I'm not there, have me paged — whatever time it is." He walked to the door with a limp that wasn't there when he first came in.

"Will you let me know what happens with Elizabeth?" I said.

"Of course." He turned to leave, but stopped. "Look, I know it was hard for you to tell me all this. But no matter what happens, you did the right thing. I know it and you should too."

After he left, Dan and I sat and watched the ocean through the thick fog for several long minutes. Then he reached for my hand.

He took in a deep sigh. "Sophie," he said, "this is driving me crazy."

"I know. I know what it's doing to you." I held his hand tightly. "I'd feel the same way if things were reversed."

"What do you think of Detective Samms?" he asked.

"I think he's a pain in the tush. And what's with that moose stain? Did you see it? What is that — some manly order of elks or something?"

He laughed. "I like him."

"What's to like?"

He tilted his head. "He sized you up right away."

"No way, Dan."

"Oh yes he did. He knew exactly how to handle you."

I stood up and got my things. "For your information Daniel, your wife is an enigma to the world."

Dan and I had planned to have lunch at the local deli. I was glad it was still on. We got there in only five minutes.

I was uptight and therefore famished. I was gnawing on a breadstick and reading the menu, which I knew by heart anyway, but it was a nice accompaniment to the breadsticks. By the third one, I was on to the salad column. I ordered a chef salad without the cheese. Dan ordered a BLT, which I prayed would come with fries.

The deli was a local favorite, naturally decorated with a nautical theme. Buoys, nets and wooden sea gulls adorned the dark wooden walls. It was tacky but cozy. The waitress brought our lunch. There were fries.

"Let's talk about something cheerful," I said. "Are you going to grow something different in the garden this year?"

It was usually heavenly to be with Dan but now our undercurrent of fear and frustration was always there. How lucky I was to have met him when he took an adolescent psych course I was teaching years ago. His optimism was such a contrast to my negative always-worried way of thinking. Other than his Robert Redford looks, I'm sure his healthy positive outlook is what attracted me so much. He once gave me a sampler that his mother had made. It read, "Do not stain today's blue skies with tomorrow's clouds." And that sums up pretty well how he stays so upbeat. I watched him as he thought about the question I had just asked. It felt so good to be near him. But I knew the serenity of this lunch date wouldn't last long.

"Bamboo."

"Bamboo?"

"Bamboo. We can use the bamboo shoots in stir fries, then we can use the mature plant stalks as supports for tomatoes and cucumbers."

Nothing ever grows in Dan's garden. Well, maybe a tomato or two, and a few ears of corn. The only perennials that come back annually are woodchucks. But Dan always perseveres with never a thought of giving up. His kids in Hyannis don't know how lucky they are to have him as a guide.

During the winter, he labors over gardening catalogues and we begin another compost pile, which I detest. He keeps this clay jar in the kitchen and watches Robin and me like a sentry, lest we throw some vegetable matter in the trash instead of the jar. Not often enough, he empties it out back in the compost heap of moldy food. Both Robin and I empty our plates into the trash can when we don't think he's looking. But once he caught me tossing out some old spinach.

"What did you just do?" he said. I remember saying that to my first puppy a lot.

"I'm so sorry," I said, retrieving the gloppy greens and putting them in the jar.

"You took perfectly good nutrients and threw them out."

I hung my head in shame then tried desperately not to laugh.

We have the only kitchen which has a fruit fly population that winters over.

During late winter, he starts hundreds of seedlings under a grow light in the basement. When they start to pop up out of the soil, he's like a new mother, cooing and clucking over them. Three weeks later, when all the seedlings are dead, he plants a new batch.

It's like raising lemmings.

"Bamboo sounds most interesting, my dear." He couldn't tell if I was being sarcastic or not. I wasn't. Just patronizing.

He rolled his eyes. I grabbed a fry.

I finished my salad, making sure to clean out all the blue cheese with the remaining bread sticks. The waitress came to take our dishes. There were five French fries left on Dan's plate.

"Are you through, sir?" she asked.

"No," I answered. She left.

"I was through, Sophie."

"What about those?" I pointed to the fries.

"They're cold and greasy and you don't want them."

"Are you trying to tell me something?"

"You're always worrying about your weight. And with all the pressure, you always overdo it with food. I was just trying to help."

"Well, now I don't want them," I said.

"Sophie, please."

"You always say, 'Sophie, please,' when you want to avoid an issue," I said.

"Sophie, ple...Jesus Christ, will you give me a break?"

"I want you to tell me the truth about something," I said.

"Oh God."

I leaned over and looked him square in the eyes. "Do I look fat?"

He picked up a cold fry and poured what seemed like a half cup of ketchup on it. "No."

"I want the truth, Dan. I really mean it. I know you love me and you want the best for me. Now, I'm saying it again. Tell me the truth."

"Well." He ate a quarter of the fry. "You may have put on a few pounds lately."

I stood up. "You insensitive monster."

He pulled me back down in the chair. "Sophie, for God's sake, you've told me a million times to tell you if you've gained weight."

"But you should have known I didn't mean it!"

He threw his hands up in the air. "How was I supposed to know you didn't mean it? You know, this past month has made you even weirder than you normally are."

"Oh." I grabbed the ketchup bottle and shook it again and again until my salad bowl was half full. "Not only am I gaining ten pounds a day, but now I don't communicate right?"

He put his hands over his face and shook his head.

The waitress came by and asked if we'd like anything else. "No," I hissed at her. She sped away.

"When did you first notice?" I growled through clenched teeth.

He put his hand over mine. I snatched mine away. He put his back. "You don't want to continue this," he said.

"Oh yes I do. You started this whole thing. You better tell me now!"

"Well," he sucked in a deep breath, "when you were wearing your gray sweat pants, your rear end looked a little more spread out."

"Did I ask you for details?"

He stood up and motioned to the waitress for our check. I pulled him back down. "How much is it?"

"It'll be around twelve dollars. I have it."

"That's not what I meant."

"Let's go, Sophie."

"I want to know how much weight I've gained. I can't tell myself, since I threw out the scale."

"Okay. I must be crazy for telling you this. But it's probably about fifteen pounds."

"Words cannot say how much I hate you."

He looked up toward the heavens. I thought about the serrated steak knife on the next table.

This time he stood up and put on his coat. I stood too.

"I never want you to tell me this again no matter how many times I ask you to tell me. Do you fully understand this?"

He didn't answer me, but I was certain he understood.

Chapter Five

Dan dropped me off at my office before going to the center. Lately, his brow was always furrowed. I was usually able to read him and tell what he was thinking. And now of course he's miserable. I suppose his feelings of helplessness in terms of not being able to make things right have made him depressed. His reason to be — his desire to save things and save people — seemed beyond his reach with me. And although I knew it wasn't rational, that has sent my guilt scale through the roof.

I was just in time for my two o'clock appointment with my obsessive compulsive patient — Charlie Downey. I checked with the answering service and found that there was a message from Detective Samms. I dialed the station right away and got him.

"No one was home at the Darbys' house," he said.

"Oh God."

"You have any idea where they might have gone? A bar for instance?"

"No." I took a deep breath. "I only know Elizabeth said she'd go to her sister's in Quincy, but I'm not sure she meant it. Wait a minute. I have that number written down in my appointment book." I gave him the number.

"Call you later," he said.

"When?" I asked, but he had already hung up.

Now more February rains railed against the window. A fitting sound. A funereal drumbeat.

I could hear Charlie in the waiting room, ten minutes early for his appointment. Without a secretary, I relied on the sound of the waiting room door, which slammed shut when someone came in because the building was so drafty. I looked out the window. It was high tide. Five

67

red-breasted mergansers were diving for fish. Only one was successful in capturing its silvery prey, but a huge opportunistic seagull swooped down and grabbed it out of his beak.

I got up and opened my door and greeted Charlie. He came in, took out a tissue from a small package of Kleenex in his pocket and wiped off the door handle before closing it. Then he got another Kleenex and wiped the arms and seat of the chair before sitting down.

Poor Charlie, just twenty-eight years old, had been diagnosed with Obsessive Compulsive Disorder when he was seventeen. Since then, he's been in therapy with a multitude of psychiatrists. His days were primarily focused around cleanliness rituals. He worked out of his home as a computer data analyst, connecting with his company via the phone line and modem. He has never married and still lives with his mother. His main goal in therapy was not to stop his symptoms. It was to leave his mother.

He was the hand-washer we all read about in our training. Sometimes he needed to scrub his raw hands fifty times a day. He was a very sweet looking man who wore wire rimmed glasses, and had light brown hair that he kept closely cropped. He always came to our sessions wearing a perfectly ironed three-piece business suit.

Charlie's obsessive-compulsiveness increased proportionately to his stress. And now that he was thinking of leaving his mom, his stress was way up there. I would never try to talk him out of his rituals. They were protective mechanisms for him, decreasing his anxiety.

"Do you think my mother would get sick if I left her? What if she died?"

"I don't think that would make her die, Charlie. And if she did get sick, it wouldn't mean that it was because of something you did. Have you actually told her you were thinking of leaving? She may be more understanding than you think. She may think it's perfectly normal for you to want your own place."

"No, I haven't said anything yet. I hate to hurt her."

"Well, most parents feel sad when their children leave. But most know it's only right. You might consider giving her a chance."

The button on the cuff of his left sleeve was undone. For Charlie, this aberration was equivalent to sitting there naked. He saw me glance at his sleeve. He looked at it and turned beet red, then he awkwardly buttoned it. We were silent as he carefully touched each button on his shirt and then each cuff again. Then he checked the button on his pants. His dilemma was what to do with the buttons on his shirt that were tucked into his pants. I knew he couldn't rest until he checked them. He was getting redder by the minute, with a pathetic little smile on his face.

"Charlie," I said, "I know that this may seem a bit unusual, but I've been having trouble with the little refrigerator in the waiting room and I just thought I heard it make a funny noise. Rather than sitting here being worried about it, would you excuse me while I take a second to check on it?"

His flush visibly lessened. "Please," he encouraged, "please, Doctor Green. I know exactly what that's like. Check it as many times as you need to."

I closed the office door behind me so he could check his other buttons. When I returned, he looked significantly more relaxed.

We noticed the movement of the group of mergansers. They skidded away on the water as the *Pilgrim* slowly chugged into the harbor, making its way to its berth. The husky was in his proud position on the bow. The captain looked up at us briefly then expertly maneuvered his boat to rest against the dock. We needed this break but the intensity quickly resumed.

"I think I will tell her tonight that I'm just thinking about finding my own place. See how she reacts to it."

"That's a good idea — feeling her out at first. Then, over a while, you could slowly let it sink in."

The captain was now standing on the dock. His dog remained on the boat ignoring his master's hand commands to jump from the boat to the pier. I guess the husky just didn't want the trip to end. The captain was smiling at his pup.

The ship's clock chimed. Charlie took a deep breath. He went to the door then wiped the handle before opening it and leaving.

I felt exhausted. I checked the service. No call from Elizabeth.

By the time I got home, all I wanted to do was watch Rhoda reruns, but we had to go to my folks' house for dinner. I checked the service again and gave them my parents' number to call if anybody called me…"anybody at all," I told them. Where the hell was Elizabeth and what the hell was Detective Samms doing about any of this?

It was about a twenty minute drive to their home in New Seabury. Dan drove. The roads were wet and icy. The driving was tough. I looked over at him. He seemed preoccupied with more than the driving and the drama at my office. "What's going on?" I asked, reaching over and brushing his pretty blond hair from his forehead.

We drove past estuaries and coves that in the summer are packed with sailboats but were now dramatically empty. The tide was at its lowest point of the day. I always thought of evening low tides in February as the Cape's most mysterious time, when darkness fell early and the water in the coves was black and still.

Dan didn't answer me right away. He was lost in thought. After a moment he said, "There's this kid at the center." I continued to brush his hair, hoping he'd let me in on what was going on. Normally we didn't spend much time talking shop. We had made a pact of sorts early on not to. Otherwise it would take up too much of our time together and we'd never get away from work. But there were times, of course, when things needed to be shared. "He doesn't talk," he went on to say. "Elective Mutism. He *can* talk. He just won't."

"I've heard of that. But I've never seen a patient with that diagnosis."

Robin's ears perked up. "Why is he like that, Dad?"

Dan shrugged his shoulders. "I don't know. He's been coming in for about a month now and he hasn't said a word. I'm worried about him."

"Can you call his parents?" I said.

"I have. I met them last week. They're wonderful people. That's the troubling thing."

"Well you know as well as I do that what really goes on in a family could be very different from what they show the outside world."

"I know."

"Do the other kids make fun of him?" Robin asked.

"They mimic him behind his back."

"Can't you stop them, Dad?"

"Only when I see them do it."

We pulled up to my folks' house. Like most Cape homes, it was made of gray wooden shingles. It wasn't nearly as fancy as most of the estates in ritzy New Seabury, but it had the lovely trademark driveway made of crushed white clam shells. We parked and went inside. When my mother saw me, she knew things weren't right.

"You don't look good," she said. She took off her glasses and peered closely at my face. "You look tired. What's the matter?"

"Nothing," I answered. I silently thanked God that they obviously heard nothing about the swastika.

My folks are both under five and a half feet tall, with thinning gray hair and all too quickly thinning bodies. Dad is a retired clothing wholesaler. Mother ran the house and everything else.

"I'm your mother and I know something's wrong. You've got more of those little spidery lines around your eyes." She looked closer at me. "And around your mouth too, now that we're on the subject." Her dining room, though formal, had a Cape Cod flavor to it. The border on the wallpaper was of cranberries. She had an antique wooden cranberry scoop on the dining room table as a centerpiece.

"Mother, please," I said. "I'm fine, just aging. Let's not talk about me. Okay?"

"What's wrong with her, Dan?" she asked. "She looks like dreck."

"She's just working too hard. That's all," he said.

"Mother," I said, "I'm really okay. I'm just seeing some tough people. Some of my patients are quite disturbed."

"What did you expect, specializing in psychiatry, people who need their bunions sawed off?"

The five of us sat at the dining room table eating her brisket, her butter-basted quartered potatoes, and her green beans with slivered almonds. Even Robin was eating.

I wanted to relax, but I kept thinking about Detective Samms and Elizabeth and all the rest of it.

"All right, we'll change the subject," she said. "I want you to talk to your father about the maid. He fired her."

Acting under the pretense that I was an adult I said, "Mother, please. You do this all the time. Whatever the problem is, it's between you two."

A waft of guilt floated gently over my head, tapping ever so lightly to come in. Never be assertive with your mother. It absolutely, one hundred percent, never in a million years, pays off.

"Why did you fire the maid, Milton?" Ah Dan, so naive at times.

"Because she was stealing," my mother said.

"How did you know she was stealing?" Dan asked.

71

"You just know these things," she said.

Throwing my empathic counselor self out the window I said, "I really don't see the point in discussing this. It's over and done with."

There was indeed a moment when nobody talked.

"Fine, Sophie," my mother said. "Just like a psychiatrist, you don't do anything."

Robin looked ready to crawl under the table.

"Ma, I'm sorry," I said. "I dealt with some very difficult patients today."

"Who do you expect to walk into your office? A bunch of plumbers?"

I silently repeated my mantra to myself, the melodious repetition of the words "marshmallow spread."

"All right, Ma. I do understand." I mustered my compassion. "You're upset because you feel that Dad is taking over a job that belongs to you."

"Are you listening, Milton? Wait until I tell her about the sliders you ordered."

Here I was, right in the middle again.

"I'm just trying to help out, Esther," Dad said, continuing to eat.

"No one can talk to your father," she said. "When he makes up his mind, you might as well keep your mouth shut. It's like fighting town hall."

"City," my father said between bites.

"What city?" my mother said.

"City Hall, Esther."

"What does that have to do with anything?" She turned to me. "You see what I mean? Your father doesn't make any sense. You should call Doctor Cohen, Milton." She passed the plate of steaming buttery potatoes past me to Dan, who took seconds.

I whispered to him, "If you don't scoop four of those things on my plate within the next three seconds, I'm going to shave your head in your sleep."

He scooped.

Dessert was sponge cake topped with strawberries and whipped cream. As my mother was serving, she asked me how my diet was going. I told her I hadn't realized I was on one.

"You could stand to lose a good ten pounds, Sophie," she said.

I piled a mound of whipped cream on my cake.

"Ma," I said, "I'd appreciate it if we could talk about something else."

"You always want to talk about something else."

Whoops. Another dollop of whipped cream landed on the cake.

After dessert, my mother and I took care of the dishes while the others watched television. I ate the last potato off the serving dish, then spooned the remaining whipped cream into my mouth. She took the bowl out of my hand and put it in the dishwasher.

"I can tell something's the matter," she said. I looked at her with love in my heart. She had become so little in the last few years. "You know you can call me day or night if there's something you want to talk about."

"Thanks, mamala." I reached out to hug her, but she was too busy to see. She turned away and started the dishwasher and I...well...I let the moment pass.

When it was time to go, she handed me the leftover sponge cake wrapped in foil and indicated twice that it was for my daughter.

On the ride home, my left hand found a tiny opening in the silver foil around the cake. And like a miracle, the foil parted. We pulled in our driveway. The motion detector light went on. It lit up the faint outline of the swastika.

I went inside and called the service from upstairs. There was still no word from Elizabeth or Samms. While changing into my nightshirt, I put on the local cable station. I sidled up to Dan and suggested he'd feel a whole lot better about his day if he gave me a really great deep-muscle back massage.

"How can you act like everything's perfectly normal?" he said.

"What do you want me to do?" I grabbed his hands. We sat on the bed. The TV was still on. Dan got up. "You watch television," he said. "I'm going downstairs."

I ran after him. "Dan! Please don't shut me out."

He stood in the doorway and hung his head. "I'm pissed off at whoever's doing this, because he's doing this to us, not just you."

"I know." I touched the back of his neck.

"I have something to tell you," he said. "I've decided to send Robin to my brother's house in Hingham. I've already called him and told him everything."

"How could you do this without talking to me?"

"Because I knew you'd try to stop me."

"Sending Robin away won't do anything to save her. Carl could find her if that's what he wants. But I'm the one he wants. Not you. Not Robin. I want her here. She'll be safe in this house. I want to be able to see her. I don't want her to go away." And then I couldn't stop crying.

I expected him to comfort me but instead he went downstairs.

I lay down in bed. I could hear Dan opening the door to the wood stove and loading it with wood for the night. I was too tired to even take off my slippers. I turned off the TV and turned on the radio. And then I heard it: "An Eastham woman was found dead in her home tonight, apparently the victim of a stabbing. Her name is being withheld, pending notification of her family."

I was motionless — paralyzed. And then I screamed, "Dan! Oh Dan!" And I let out a horrible wail.

He came running up the stairs and grabbed me in his arms.

"What is it?" I was shaking.

Breathing heavily, I told him what I heard.

"Are you sure it's her?" he asked.

"I don't know, Dan. I don't know," I said, my hands trembling. "Dan, I'm falling apart! Tell me you won't send Robin away right now. I can't take it!"

"I don't know, Sophie."

"Will you call Samms for me? Find out if it's Elizabeth?"

"Of course. Don't jump to conclusions right away," he said. "It could be anybody."

You let another one die, Sophie.

"I'm going downstairs for some sherry," I said. "Will you come with me and call from there?" I reached out and took his arm.

We went downstairs to the kitchen. He called the detective at the station. The person who answered the phone said they would have him paged.

Five minutes later, Samms called saying he'd be right over. Dan didn't ask him the obvious over the phone and I was glad to put it off. I poured myself a second glass of sherry. Robin had gone to bed, thank God, and had not been a part of the commotion. Dan and I went to the couch and waited.

A cold blast of February air surrounded me as Samms came in the door. All I needed to see was the expression on his face. He didn't have to say a word.

But like a hopeful little girl, I still looked at him questioningly. He nodded yes.

I couldn't help the torrent of tears. "But you said you went there and no one was home!" I cried.

"No one was," he said. He winced as he took off his herringbone coat. He put it over the arm of the couch and painstakingly sat down. "About an hour ago, a neighbor called because they could hear her screaming."

"But where were they this afternoon?" I asked hysterically.

Dan put his arm around me.

"That's not really what we're concerned with right now." Samms spoke softly.

"Is Carl in jail?"

"No, he's not."

"Then where is he?"

"We don't know. There's an APB out for him, but he was gone when we got to the house and he could be anywhere by now."

I looked around my living room, everything so deceivingly comfortable. My lovely life on old Cape Cod. It's what everybody dreams of. And now it's ruined.

"How could I have let this happen?" I was still crying.

"You didn't do it," Samms said. "You know who's responsible here."

"Don't talk to me like that!" I lashed out. "What makes you such an authority? How do you know there wasn't something else I could have done?" I put my face in my hands. Dan came to console me but I turned away.

Samms didn't answer me, probably knowing that there was nothing he could say to convince me I wasn't at fault. He rubbed his knee. Then he slowly got up from the couch.

"Will you tell me what you find out?" I said.

"Of course."

"And Carl, he could be anywhere?"

He nodded. He shook both of our hands before he left. He patted my shoulder in an ever-so-slight gesture of affection.

Dan went with me upstairs to bed. The sherry had shrouded my pain for now. I lay on my back looking at the moon through the lacy curtain. I could hear Dan's breathing slow down in sleep. Then I turned on my side and faced him. He had moonlight on his face. I touched his mouth and he opened his eyes.

"I'm sorry I woke you," I said.

He outlined my face with his finger.

We looked at each other while our eyes took turns closing and opening. He fell back asleep, and I let him stay that way.

The early morning sun lit up the space on the pillow where Dan's head should have been. He needed his space. And I needed more sleep.

There was a conference I had to attend today at the Sheraton in Hyannis. Normally, I liked these things, but today I couldn't remember what "normal" was. The topic was eating disorders, and I sure didn't need to bone up on that. I stayed in bed for a while thinking about Elizabeth. I was torturing myself with "if onlys" and the more I stayed in bed, the worse it got. I forced myself to get up, shower and go downstairs.

After two cups of coffee with whole cream—who are we kidding with this half and half business—I felt ready to face a room full of therapists.

I drove myself to the Sheraton after a fight about it with Dan. Having him take me everywhere was making me feel like an invalid, and I needed to operate some controls. Our other truck was out of the shop so he could get to the center. I hated that thing. It's a twenty year old Ford with a cab up front that fits two people if the passenger doesn't mind the draft from the hole in the floorboard. It has a truck bed in the back that holds vital things like cow manure and sea weed. I had a license plate made for it that says "Dan's truck." I call it that because I won't get in it.

I was wearing my good white wool suit, which had become tighter lately. I wasn't so frightened about going to the conference alone. Carl wouldn't come after me in a room filled with a few hundred people.

Today's seminar set up included a beckoning table of coffee and muffins for the attendees. Looking around, I had the feeling of being watched. I poured a cup of java and forced myself to say hello to a nice looking bearded young man.

"Hi." I shook his hand. "My name is Sophie Green."

"Hello, I'm Doctor Garrison."

Oh boy. A down to earth type. I noticed his watch. In place of each numeral was the word "NOW." I thought I'd puke.

I asked, "Are you a specialist in eating disorders or do you just come here for the carbohydrates?" What a riot I can be.

He raised one eyebrow. I've never been able to figure out how people do that. I can however cross one eye, which Robin thinks is disgusting but Dan thinks is funny.

The speaker spent the first part of the morning talking about binge eating disorder and the psychology behind compulsive eating.

During the mid-morning break, the hotel staff put out an enormous spread of bagels, banana bread, fruit, blueberry muffins, sweet rolls and coffee cake.

No one touched a thing.

I piled my plate with one of everything except fruit, topping any flat surface with whipped butter. I put my plate on the table and dissected the muffin, slicing it into four pieces so I could spread a knifeful of cream cheese on each. When a lump of cream cheese fell onto my chest, someone handed me a cloth napkin. I looked up to see Eliot Wohlman.

I took the napkin and removed the glop from my blouse, but wasn't quite sure what to do with it, so I balled it up in the napkin.

"How are you?" he said. I hated to admit he was good looking in a rather seasoned MASH movie star sort of way.

"Just peachy," I said. Eliot was definitely a binge eating deterrent. Who could luxuriate in banana bread with a madman in your face? I put my plate down, but not before wrapping up the onion bagel in my cream cheese filled napkin. It's tough finding good bagels on the Cape.

"I was sorry to hear about your patient," he said.

"How do you know anything about it?" I felt a piece of blueberry in the space between my front teeth.

"A murder, Sophie. How could I not know about it?"

"But how did you know it was one of my patients?" I took a toothpick to the blueberry and got it out. Maybe this would make him go away.

"Cape Cod's a small town."

"That's not an answer. Who told you?"

"Hold it. Everybody's known about Carl Darby for years. He's been in trouble since he was a kid. He's even ratted on his pals to the police to get himself off the hook."

He took a long sip of coffee. "I got a call yesterday from Wallace Samms," he said. "He wanted my professional opinions about your situation." People were milling all around us. "I said that in my opinion you're dealing with somebody who's not very bright. Everything he's been doing is almost childish. I mean, silly sea worms? I think there's a good chance Carl's your nemesis. It's too bad they haven't found him."

"How do I know it isn't you, Eliot?" I couldn't believe Samms was relying on his opinions.

"How can I convince you I didn't paint the swastika or do any of the things you think I did? You know it all adds up to Carl."

"Okay. Tell me the brilliant diagnostic information you gave Detective Samms." I looked up at him but it hurt my neck. It's hard to be intimidating when you're looking up.

"If you really want to hear, I'll tell you," he said.

"I'm champing at the bit." I unwrapped the bagel and took a huge bite. The cream cheese that had originated on my blouse before traveling to the napkin, was now on the end of my chin. None of this was helping my credibility.

"The only reason I am not walking away right now is because I'm worried about you," he said while picking up a napkin for me from the table. I grabbed it and cleaned my chin. "Judging from Carl's style, you're in a great deal of danger. He's basic and primitive. And primitive responses can be the most impulsive."

"Talk about primitive and impulsive. Don't you have a wife and daughter at home?"

"Look," he said, "I know there's a strain in our relationship and I know why. It must be awkward to know things about me both professionally and personally. Please try not to judge me."

"Too late for that."

"Well," he shrugged his shoulders, "I told Samms that I'd be glad to consult with him at any time."

How could Samms treat Eliot as a consultant and not a suspect? If

Samms wasn't going to find out the truth from Eliot, then I was sure as hell going to try.

"Sophie." He gave me a phony "sympathetic" look.

"Don't start with that look, Eliot. I want to know where you were Monday morning before ten o'clock."

He laughed. "I'm not going to answer that."

"Wouldn't life be a tad easier for you if I wasn't seeing your girlfriend? Nobody would be sitting in my office week after week telling me sordid details about you, would they?"

"Watch it, Sophie. You're crossing the line of privileged communication."

"Oh no, I'm not. I'm just saying you're right. Cape Cod is such a small town. Everybody knows everybody. What would the hospital board have to say about your affair? Not to mention your poor unsuspecting wife."

"Are you threatening me?"

"Am *I* threatening *you*? Give me a fucking break."

"Sit down, Sophie." He motioned toward a couch.

"You're always telling me to sit down," I said. "It's time to go back to the lecture." I turned away.

He grabbed my arm. "You know a lot about me and probably don't approve of some of my actions, but you act like I'm some kind of monster. You think it could be me that's doing these things to you and you're wrong."

I pulled my arm away, then stood silently as he turned and went back into the meeting room.

On the ride home, all I could think about was food. There'd better still be a frozen Hershey bar with almonds in the freezer, or somebody was going to pay. I had already finished my bagel during the part of the conference when attendees were arguing about sugar and white flour being responsible for war. I drove home on Route 28. This section leading out of Hyannis had lost its Cape Cod naturalness and instead was lined with strip malls and fake quaint Ye Olde Real Estate agencies.

I missed having Dan with me. I missed the assumption of safety I felt when he was around. Of course, that assumption was an illusion, I discovered, when I was a little girl of forty.

There was a pick-up truck two cars behind me I was trying to ignore.

"Thanks, God," I said out loud. "The day I'm on my independence kick, you stick that truck in the picture. Nice touch."

Now it was directly behind me. Oh Christ, what if it was Carl? I didn't want the driver to know I was aware of him. They say you can become a victim just by acting like one, but that's nonsense. Some things in this life really are arbitrary. With a quick glance in my side mirror, I could tell that the driver was a white man. His face was either dirty or scarred.

I was about a half a mile from the turn off to my road and he was coming closer. I wasn't sure if Dan was home so I was afraid to go to the house. When I came to our street, I drove past it. The pick-up stayed with me. I was a few blocks from a Mobil station up ahead.

I reached down between the seats for the phone to call Dan.

I fumbled with the black casing that holds the phone. I passed the Mobil station.

Damn. The case was empty. Someone had taken the phone.

My breathing got faster, so I chanted some mind/body thing I heard on Oprah. "My breath is always with me. There's a peaceful place in me that nothing can touch no matter what."

Right.

"SHIT! FUCK! SHIT! FUCK!" There, that was better.

The pick-up was close. I decided to turn around in the next street and go back to the Mobil station. I pulled in a narrow road, and began to back up.

He blocked me. If I went straight, he'd block me at the dead end. I had to stop.

The driver got out of the car and approached me. Panicking, I locked the doors, and sat there like a rabbit about to be shot.

Carl Darby's face appeared at my window.

"What do you want?" I yelled.

"Get out of the car."

I blasted the horn.

He reached down and picked up a rock. He was about to smash the window when I yelled, "Okay, okay!"

I unlocked the door with numb fingers and slid out of the car. I leaned against it to stop the trembling.

"You killed Elizabeth," he said.

"Carl, I…"

"She was happy before she started seeing you."

"No, she wasn't. She was never happy."

"You ruined our marriage. You ruined our lives. Who do you think you are that you can just tell everyone what to do?" His breath smelled of beer. "You told her to leave me. She told me so herself."

"She told me about the knife."

"But I was sorry I done that."

I looked around for an escape route and saw none. I thought of Robin and Dan and how desperately I loved them and I prayed I would see them again. Oh, God. Please. Help me get away. Please!

"She used to laugh before she came to see you. She used to listen to me. We'd party every night."

"But she was unhappy."

He took a step away from me. "You think I'm to blame for that?"

"I didn't tell her that. She had a tough life before you. Her father was a sick man who would take things out on her. She blamed herself for everything he did, and she blamed herself when you would get angry at her."

I could swear I saw tears in his eyes.

"She was a good girl, Carl," I said, softening my voice. "She was beautiful both inside and outside."

There were definitely tears. I had to use this to get out of here.

"Please let me go," I whispered.

"No."

"Carl. You can tell the authorities you weren't in your right mind." I knew the words insanity defense would set him off again.

"I wasn't in my right mind. I killed the one person I needed." He wiped his eyes with the back of his hand. He opened his other hand and dropped the rock. "You don't know how I feel. You can't know how bad I feel."

"You've lost the one person who gave meaning to your life."

"I tried to make it work. My biggest problem was that I loved her too much."

"I know."

"What am I supposed to do now? I've got nothing." He looked around, as if unsure of where he was.

"You'll do the right thing. I know you will."

"I'm not thinking straight right now. I...uh."

I touched his shoulder and said good-bye. With the grace of God, Carl would stay in this trance state until I left.

I got in the car, talking the whole time. "She really was beautiful, Carl. You were right to love her as much as you did. And knowing her like I did, I can guarantee you she would forgive you if she could."

And I knew in my heart she would have done just that.

I slowly started the car and backed up around his truck. From my rear view, I could see him still standing where he was. He was looking at the ground. His shoulders were heaving.

I made it home in under five minutes.

Without taking the time to explain to Dan, I ran upstairs to the bedroom phone and reached Detective Samms. I told him what had just happened. He asked me if I drove straight home after the incident. I said I had. He said that wasn't smart.

"I'll send a patrolman over there," he said, "but don't answer your door unless you know who it is."

Dan came into the bedroom while I was on the phone. He sat on the bed and began lacing up his boots.

"I'm going to look up Carl's address and go over to his house," he said when I hung up.

"Don't you dare," I said.

"I can't just sit here and do nothing."

"It's better than leaving us alone. What if something happened to you?"

"He doesn't know what I look like."

"Says who?"

Robin knocked on the door.

"Come in, sweets," I said. Dan went downstairs. "Don't you dare leave!" I yelled after him.

When I didn't hear a response, I ran down the stairs and saw him putting on his coat.

"Dan." I grabbed his arm. "Please don't do this."

"I have to do something. I'm going crazy here."

"I know. But if you get hurt, what am I going to do? Please, with everything in me, I'm begging you not to do this." I started to cry. He looked at the ceiling.

"What's going on?" Robin yelled from upstairs.

"I've got to go to her," I said. "Dan…"

He slowly took off his coat.

I ran up the stairs. Back in my bedroom, I found her searching through the contents of my jewelry box, not looking at me. I don't think there's an adolescent alive who has mastered the art of eye contact. Probably because they're always lying.

"I know something's going on, Mom, and I want to know the truth."

I looked away.

"Okay, Robin. I want to say it's not a big deal, but I won't." For one second in the universe, we looked at each other. Then I turned away. "Um…well, I've been having trouble with someone at the office. I've narrowed it down to two people. We have a detective working on it, and I'm going to have a panic button installed under my desk."

She had stopped playing with the jewelry and just stood there with her mouth open.

"We're going to have a burglar alarm installed here too," I went on. "One that will notify the police immediately if there's a problem."

"When were you planning on telling me about that?"

It's horrible to be embarrassed in front of your own daughter.

"I was just trying to play it all down, I guess. Anyway, lots of people are getting them these days."

"Is someone trying to kill you, Mom?"

Ah, teenagers. Never any fluff.

"It's not going to happen," I said. "Not with all the protection."

"Well now I feel a whole lot better," she said sarcastically.

"Robin, it's perfectly normal for all of us to be nervous about this. I'm so sorry that I didn't tell you all about it sooner." And I was. "Honey, I think you should stay at your uncle's house for awhile."

"I don't want to." She was about to cry.

"I know, but it would be safer for you to be somewhere else."

"Maybe I could help you, somehow. I don't want to go anywhere. That would be a million times worse." She came and sat next to me on the bed. "Please don't make me go."

I gave her a hug. She stiffened.

"I'll think about it, but only on one condition." I made my tone playful. "You make dinner tonight."

She got up to leave. "You'll hate that. You'll hover, you always do." I could tell she was trying to match my playfulness, for my sake. "You take the kitchen way too seriously, in case you haven't noticed."

"I promise I won't go into the kitchen until you call me."

She left the room. I leaned back against the pillow and closed my eyes, listening to the sound of my breathing finally slowing down. When will this end? How will it end?

Twenty minutes later I sneaked down the stairs to investigate the source of a sour burning smell. I went into the kitchen.

"I knew it Mom," she said. "Have you ever once kept a promise?"

"Not that I can remember."

"We're having cheeseburgers, made out of real hamburger, not made out of a turkey," she said.

I sat at the table and tried not to think about that.

"We're having real cheese on the burgers, not that fake orange stuff."

"It's not fake. It's just no-fat."

"Well, this isn't."

Dan came in and sat next to me. I squeezed his hand.

Robin heated what looked like a gallon of oil in a deep frying pan.

"Scared, Mom?" She didn't wait for an answer.

I got up and threw together some salad so that the cholesterol globules would have something to cling to. Finally, I felt a little better. I had to bring some normalcy into our home, even if it was only for this one meal.

The two of them took modest helpings of fries. I took a dockworker's serving. On top of my cheeseburger I piled a slice of Bermuda onion, a slice of tomato, a tablespoonful each of mayo, ketchup and mustard. I topped it all with relish that I sprinkled with bacon bits. I pushed the bits into the relish with my fingers so they wouldn't fall off.

They were both looking at me with incredulous expressions.

"Watch this," I said, and picked up the entire masterpiece without spilling one drop of anything.

Dan seemed to need to lighten up the mood as well. He said to Robin, "Let's bet her ten dollars she can't get that thing into her mouth just once, without dripping something."

"You're on, Dad," she said, and shook his hand.

84

Keeping my eyes focused on the burger, I dramatically inched it toward the target. I could hear Robin giggling.

"No fair," I said, still not taking my eyes off it. "No giggling, Robin."

They both started snorting in a way that always got me going. They fed on each others' noises, sounding like a barnyard of lunatic animals.

A giggle was beginning in my throat. The burger trembled in my hands.

"Not fair, you two lousy rotten stinkfaces." With a valiant thrust, I plunged the burger into my mouth. Not one drop fell on the table.

"I did it!" I glowered in their direction. I held my hand out for the ten dollars. Dan reluctantly gave it to me.

We never did bother with the salad.

After dinner, I checked with the service to find I had only one call.

"It's from a Carl Darby," the operator said.

"What did he say?"

"He said, 'Just say to her she tricked me.'"

"That was all he said?"

"Yes, Doctor Green."

Chapter Six

Against everybody's better judgment, I decided to go to Elizabeth's funeral. About thirty people were assembled in the little church in Eastham. Dan wanted to come, but I didn't feel that was right. I wanted to say "good-bye" the same way it always was. Just Elizabeth and me. I wasn't worried for my safety. There was a policeman at the church and I was sure there would be one at the cemetery too.

I think of Eastham as pure Cape Cod. There are very few residents compared to the rest of the Cape. I usually love coming to this remote part of the peninsula, where each view is either of the ocean or sand dunes or cranberry bogs.

I could see Elizabeth's parents in the front pew, and probably that was her sister there too. The few strands of red in her mother's gray hair made me overwhelmingly sad.

The service was short. Our eyes were on Elizabeth's white casket. The minister talked about forgiveness and about untimely death and about the importance of every life, no matter how short it might be.

The small cemetery with about a hundred white gravestones was behind the church. I watched as six pallbearers carried her heavy casket. I followed to see them place it on the metal bars above her grave. I didn't see the name Darby on nearby gravestones. Apparently her parents were able to have her buried with their family.

Finally, in death, Elizabeth had gotten away.

I wanted to say something at the casket. I needed to express what was simmering inside me, but her parents and her sister stayed long after anyone else, and I had to leave. I slowly walked away, never getting the chance to apologize to Elizabeth like I so needed to do.

I could see the dunes over Cape Cod Bay from the little hill the church was on. There was a panoramic view of the ocean. I thought of the early settlers burying their dead in this cemetery and walking away seeing the same view I was seeing.

I got in the truck and began driving. As I passed deep purple cranberry bogs, I felt the awareness that they would still be here long after I'm gone. The beauty of the Cape — the bogs, the wild beach roses in June — all the things that attracted me would outlast me. I usually find that depressing but today found it somehow comforting.

I looked for pussy willows on my ride. I needed to see the white fluffy buds that promised a new beginning. Alongside a marsh on the left, I spotted a big bush full of them. I pulled off and parked. The golden marsh would be flooded at high tide but the bush wasn't too far in and the tide was pretty low.

The wetness of the marsh didn't bother me. I had my dress boots on and they could take the moisture. I walked over to the bush. I felt a soft bud in my fingers.

It wasn't your fault, Sophie.

All deaths bring up thoughts of past losses. I saw Jeremy in my mind. He was in my bedroom, laughing though his life would be shut down in the next twenty seconds.

I should have gotten him away from the window.

But he was just playing, I said back to myself.

I started to cry, standing there in the marsh.

I should have known it was dangerous, I thought. He was acting so hyper — playing stupid kid games — teasing me and scaring me by leaning out of the window.

You have to forgive yourself. You loved Jeremy and you cared about Elizabeth and Jeanne. You did your best.

But I didn't. They died.

You can't carry around these expectations of yourself anymore. You can't save everybody.

I broke off a large bunch of pussy willows and buried my face in their softness.

"I'm so sorry, Elizabeth." I wept into the bouquet.

At a quarter to one, I pulled into the parking lot at my office.

I saw three patients, then drove ten minutes to Dan's center in

Hyannis. I was hoping, since it was the end of the day, he'd want to have a drink with me somewhere. I parked next to the yellow building and went inside. I didn't see him at his desk near the front door so I walked further until I got to the activities room. The door was opened a little and I could see him sitting on a bench talking to a boy. Their backs were to me. I didn't want to interrupt.

"But everybody else does it," I heard the boy say.

"But it's against the law," Dan said back.

"The law's stupid. You can drink and smoke cigarettes. What's the difference?"

"It's not a matter of whether or not the law is right and wrong. If you know something's illegal and you do it anyway then you're risking a lot."

"I'm not going to drop dead from smoking a joint."

Dan was so patient. He was being straight without being accusatory. No kids got on the defensive when they talked to him. They didn't need to. Dan was on their side and they knew it.

"I'm not talking about what pot does or doesn't do to you. You could wind up in jail or at least on probation and you'll have a record."

They boy laughed nervously. "Only if I'm caught."

"There's no guarantee you won't get caught. Do you want to take that kind of chance with your life?"

Most people would have made a declaration rather than asking a question. The way Dan dealt with kids is that he left their decisions up to them, or at least he made it look that way.

He was wearing his favorite sweatshirt. It had a picture of a great blue heron standing on the bank of a marsh on the back. Underneath were the words, "Keep the Cape Alive and Well." He bought it from a nature group concerned with the water pollution from over-development. That was another one of Dan's many causes that he felt passionate about.

The boy never answered Dan's question. They both turned around when I accidentally made the floor squeak while I shifted my position. Dan got up and came over to me. "See you tomorrow, Bob," he said as the boy walked passed me. With a wonderful smile he said to me, "What are you doing here? I didn't expect you."

"I thought you might like to go to Jake's for a drink."

"I can't. I've got a meeting in a half an hour." He kissed my forehead. "How did it go at the funeral? You all right, Soph?"

"I can't really answer that right now. We'll talk about it later when I've gotten away from it a little." I gave him a forehead kiss back. Then I gave him a real kiss — a long one. "That's okay about the drink," I said. "I'll head home. But we could make a date, you know, and go out. We haven't been to dinner in ages. You might even get lucky afterwards."

He laughed. We walked to my truck which was parked next to Dan's piece of dreck. "I'll be home as soon as I can," he said.

Robin wasn't at the house when I got there. I took some kindling from the copper wash basin and started a small fire in the wood stove.

In less than five minutes, she came in the door. Ignoring me, she stalked up the stairs.

"Robin, please come back down. I want to sit with you for a minute."

She dropped her backpack and jacket on the stairs, then came down and stood there. "Come sit with me on the couch." I patted the cushion.

She sat down reluctantly and faced away from me. My poor girl. Not only does she have to go through the trials of adolescence, she has to live with the terror surrounding my work.

"Let's talk, sweetheart," I said. "It's been so long since we just had a normal conversation. I feel like I don't even know my own daughter." What mother doesn't, I thought. "How are you doing, honeypie?"

"Okay, I guess."

"No really. I want to know. I love you, Robin."

She took a deep breath. Then she didn't say anything. I gave her time to think.

Finally, she spoke. "I don't want to hurt you, Mom."

"I know you don't."

"I've been thinking for a while," she said. "I want to get off Cape Cod. It's so suffocating here. I want to see California...or maybe Colorado. But I feel like you watch my every move and you'll have a heart attack if I ever go away."

I would feel terrible if she went away. She was right. I thought about my earlier words to Charlie. My response would be very important at this juncture in her young life.

"Well, Robin, every mother wants their child near them, but I know that someday it will be time for you to go."

She got up to leave. I grabbed her hand. There were tears in my eyes that I didn't want her to see, because I remembered how terrible I felt when I made my mother cry.

"I don't blame you for wanting to get off-Cape. And when you do, I'll survive. You need to know that, Robin. I won't like being away from you, but this is a part of life for every parent." I was still holding on to her hand. There was so much more to say, but I knew these moments of connection were terribly hard for her.

"What do you say we spend next Sunday in Provincetown?" I said. "Just you and me. We can go in all the boutiques. We can even go into that weirdo shop and try to guess what all the sex toys are for."

She couldn't resist a smile.

"And then we can have lunch together. We could have fried clams or kale soup. Oh..." I looked toward the heavens, "the list is endless."

But she turned away. "Sorry, Mom. I've got plans."

Children rarely know the impact of their rejections. Maybe it was better for them that way.

"I'm glad you told me what's going on," I said. Of course I hated it all. "Let's keep the dialogue open between us. Okay?"

"Sure, Mom."

The next morning, Dan drove me to the office. I couldn't talk him out of it, not that I tried too hard. When we were at the top of the stairs in my building, we saw a small piece of white paper stuck in the door. I grabbed it. There was nothing on it.

Somebody was trying to scare me to death. And doing a bang-up job of it.

My hands were shaking when I handed it to Dan. "This is too much!" I said. We went into my office and put our things down. "It's almost creepier that there's nothing written on it."

I flopped down in the chair and put my head in my hands.

"I'll take this to Samms myself," Dan said.

"Shouldn't we ask him to come here?"

"We already took it off the door. What else is there to see? I'll drop it off myself on the way to the center."

Charlie Downey was ten minutes late for his session. This was highly uncharacteristic. Even more unusual was that he had requested a second appointment for this week. He came in, wiped off the chair and sat down. He didn't have eye contact with me. We both looked out the window. Everything was in various shades of gray — the water, the pilings, the sky. The only colors we could see were the oranges and reds on the lobster buoys hanging on the boarded-up restaurant next door.

"Charlie," I said gently, "it doesn't matter to me that you were late for our session, but it's just so unlike you. Would you like to tell me why you were late?"

"Because I incorrectly estimated how much time it would take to get things organized before I came here."

He was avoiding something. I decided that getting to the specifics would be best. "Has something happened in your life that's been out of the ordinary?" I asked. There had to be some important explanation for his lateness.

"Yes," he said. "My mother died."

I was stunned at this news. "I'm so very sorry to hear that, Charlie." I wasn't surprised at his attitude. To Charlie, having a grief reaction would be equivalent to a loss of control. And loss of control was something that Charlie spent every waking hour trying to avoid.

"What happened?" I said softly.

He breathed a huge long sigh. "After our last session I told her that I was thinking of finding my own place. And…" We sat in silence for a moment. "I waited until we were having dinner, you see. I had made her favorite meal — broiled scrod and a baked potato. And she said, 'That's wonderful. I think you'll do fine on your own. And I'm sure we'll still be close so I know I'll be fine as well.' She seemed to mean it. She didn't look sad or upset." He cleared his throat, trying desperately to keep his emotions in check. "So the next morning I brought her a cup of tea — she likes Tetley's. And we sat together on the couch and watched the morning news while she drank it."

I waited for him to go on.

"At one point while she was drinking her tea she said, 'I've been thinking for a while that it would be better for you if you got out on your own. It's time, Charlie. Is there anything I can do to help you find a place?'"

He looked at me for a reply. I knew what he needed. He wanted to be certain there were no loopholes in her statements and that she was sincere in her approval. "So, even after sleeping on it, your mom was still happy for you. She definitely sounded like she thought it was a good idea."

He nodded and the questioning look on his face disappeared momentarily. "That night I made us meatloaf with mushroom gravy. She was in a good mood and she looked fine. Nothing seemed to be wrong. She finished her dinner and sat with me while I washed the dishes. We have a dishwasher but I never know if the dishes are really being cleaned so it makes more sense for me to wash them myself."

He stopped talking. I didn't push him. After a long moment, he continued, "Yesterday, she died in her sleep," he said in barely a whisper.

I knew he had somehow decided that logically it was all his fault.

"Please try not to blame yourself," I said. "You didn't do anything wrong." There was a deep guttural sound from his throat.

There were no perfect words for me to say. For a long five minutes, he sat motionless. Then he continued. "When I got up, I saw that she wasn't waiting for me on the couch to make her tea like she does every morning, so I went into her bedroom. And…there she was — still sleeping I thought. But then I looked more closely at her color — it was somewhat blue. And I picked up her hand and it was cold and she was, she was…" He wouldn't let himself cry. "I called the ambulance and they came right away but she was…"

He took out a Kleenex and covered his eyes. Then he folded it up carefully and put it back in his pocket. "How does anyone deal with this, Doctor Green?" he said with a look of deep pain on his face. "I can't take the thought of being without her."

I had always felt that leaving his mother was more of a problem for him than it would have been for his mom. The dependency issues were his, not hers. I still saw no tears — only grievous pain.

"Charlie," I said. "There's no formula to follow."

"I need help, Doctor," he said desperately. "If you don't help me — " His breathing grew faster in pace.

"What, Charlie? What were you going to just say?"

He began to answer but abruptly stopped himself.

I knew I was asking this to help control my own anxieties. Lately,

I've been imagining that everything my patients are saying might have a double meaning. Was Charlie afraid of his own impulses? Was he worried about hurting me? Did he blame me for his mother's death? Man, I'm going crazy and it's escalating at supersonic speeds. I took a deep breath and cleared my head. I forced myself to squelch my paranoia and talk to Charlie the way I normally would.

"I'm here to listen to you and talk with you, Charlie, but I know you're going to feel terrible for a while. There's no way around that. What you have to try very hard to do is to understand that your mother meant it when she said it was wonderful for you to go out on your own."

We sat for another few minutes in silence.

"What do I do with the pain?" he asked. "It's unbearable."

These questions were the biggest questions a therapist gets asked. Somehow, we're granted authority on matters of life and death.

"You just have to experience it, Charlie. There's no easy way out." I was successful in putting myself back in an appropriate therapy mode.

"But I've read that there are stages you go through."

Charlie needed to organize his grief, the way he organized everything, but it just wasn't possible.

I never could go along with characterizing the grieving process into stages. It simply wasn't true. And, it caused added depression when one found oneself out of sync with the "normal" stages of mourning. But I could certainly understand the desire to categorize the process. It would be more bearable to regulate the chaos.

I tried to answer his question. "Everyone is different and feels grief in their own ways. One doesn't do anything with the emotions, Charlie. That only makes it worse, or last longer. People shouldn't try to cover up their grief by not thinking about it." It was very hard for me to keep my fears at bay in this session. But I really was sure that Charlie wouldn't hurt me and I was just being overly paranoid. "You have to feel grief, experience it. It's part of the beauty of human existence. You'll do this all in your own time."

He looked at me. I could finally see tears behind the rimmed glasses. I said, "I can't remember where I read it, but some poet said that the deeper that grief cuts into your heart, the more joy it can contain."

He looked out at the harbor but I don't think he was focusing on anything. I could see he didn't want to speak. I was hoping he could find a tiny bit of solace in my words.

"I don't like the way I'm feeling," he said slowly.

The "oh no's" were returning to my brain, scaring me by questioning what he meant by that. I told them to go away. I was safe with Charlie.

"I know you don't like the way you're feeling," I said. "That's very understandable."

Charlie wasn't a religious man so he'd find no comfort there. He would have a tough time with his mother's death. The guilt of wanting to go out on his own would take ages for him to wade through.

I knew that my craziness was uncalled for and I felt better after convincing myself of that. Charlie's nature was good. In his own style, he would someday be at peace with this. But not for a very long time.

Not much more was said for the rest of our session. No conclusions were come to as I knew they wouldn't be. Charlie didn't walk away from the hour feeling any better. But that was only right because that was reality, and reality, after all, is what psychiatry is supposed to be about.

As he was leaving I told him he could call me if he wanted to talk before our next meeting. He didn't respond. He wiped the door handle, opened the door and left.

Later, I heard the sound of Dan in the waiting room. I couldn't wait to see him. I rushed out to him. Alongside of Dan was sitting Detective Samms.

"What's going on?" I asked.

They got up and came into the office.

Dan said, "Sophie. I did the only thing I could do to help stop this maniac from coming after us."

"What did you do?"

"I told Detective Samms about your patient, Gracie Brill. And I also went through all of your current files to see if there's somebody we haven't thought about. I knew that the detective wouldn't read them without your permission, so I made a summary of everyone and I gave him all of their names, addresses and phone numbers."

I turned my back so they couldn't see I was seething.

"You would have done the same thing," Samms said.

"There's no need to apologize for me," Dan said.

I spun around. "Dan..."

"Sophie, you weren't going to do it. I had no other choice."

"Don't give me that! You had a choice and you chose to go behind my back."

I grabbed the papers out of Samms' hand and shook them in the air. "You've violated every one of these people, Dan."

"I'm trying to save your life."

"Oh the high and mighty warrior."

"Don't talk to me like that, Sophie. You know me better."

"I thought I did."

"Let's calm down and talk about this," Samms said. I sat at my desk and the others took the chairs by the bay window. "First of all, the majority of these people won't even know about this," he said.

"And what about the minority who will?"

"I'm going to talk to four of your patients. I'll do it very diplomatically. I'll tell them that you didn't want their names released to me, but because of an investigation of certain threats made against you, I have to ask them some questions."

"Which four are you talking about?"

"One is named Jeffrey Owers. One is Joseph Angelo. One is Charlie Downey and one is Gracie Brill."

I knew Jeffrey and Joseph had criminal records because of OUIs so I wasn't surprised.

"Why do you need to speak to Charlie and Gracie?"

"Charlie Downey has a very extensive history of psychiatric treatment and —"

"And all people who see more than one psychiatrist are criminals?" I raised my eyebrows.

"Of course not. But in my opinion, his history of instability is extreme enough to warrant looking into. Are you positive you can predict his behavior?"

"Yes."

I was so frustrated. I looked out at the sea, past the harbor and to the bay. The waters were calm in the harbor, but they were rough in the open waters. A big rusty fishing trawler was rocking on the waves.

I turned back to Samms. "And Gracie Brill?" I said. I hadn't written down Eliot Wohlman's name in her file. This is precisely the reason I never write names. You never know if a judge or some other authority will order a file released. But from my description of her problems, Samms probably assumed that she's the one involved with Eliot.

"Immediately prior to seeing you, she spent a month in jail."

"No way. That's not in her records."

"Correct. But we did a background check on all of your patients. She assaulted a woman in court."

"What are you talking about?"

"Remember that doctor who lost his license because he was found guilty of molesting his patients?"

I nodded.

"Gracie was his girlfriend. She attacked one of the victims who accused him."

"Gracie would never do anything like that!"

"Well she did. And she couldn't be released unless she agreed to psychiatric care."

"You mean she's seeing me because it's been mandated?"

"That's right."

"But the court would have contacted me. Someone would have to get reports from me proving she was under my care!"

"No, that's not how it always works. She signed a document agreeing to outpatient psychotherapy. If she became violent again, then she'd need proof."

Samms stood up to leave. "Just one more thing," he said. He held up the paper that had been stuck in my door. It was wrapped in plastic. "I told you not to touch anything. You should have left this in the door."

I glared at him.

"You don't know what you're doing," I said.

"I'm doing my job and that's to protect people."

Chapter Seven

Saturday, 7:00 AM

The last thing I wanted to do was see my crazy brother and his wife, but the plans were made weeks ago, and I would have felt too guilty canceling. Mark and Rosie were coming over for brunch. I put on my blue sweat suit with vertical pink stripes. Then I organized a platter of bagels, lo-cal cream cheese, and no-salt lox.

I kept looking out the back door. A thick soupy fog was descending over Dan's rickety grape arbor. It was a beautiful sight in the summer. The grape bunches looked like a still life painting for about a day until the robins found them.

I could barely make out the pine and holly trees that encircle our yard. But I kept thinking they were perfect places for someone to hide behind.

I'm going nuts.

Mark and Rosie are superbrains. Both are electrical engineers and have worked for the same firm for the last eight years. Mark is forty-five and Rosie is thirty-seven. So far they have no children. I wondered if Jeremy's death was a factor in that. Mark dealt with our brother's death by burying it, I think. Soon after it happened, he spent most of his time putting together projects in his room. He had kits of ships in bottles that he'd spend hours working on. My folks were more concerned with me since I couldn't stop crying about Jeremy for weeks, maybe months.

It's hard to believe that my brother and I are from the same womb.

I worry about disease and death.

He worries about appliances.

Mark focuses on buying new appliances with the same intensity normal people do when they discuss having children. At last month's brunch, the issue was their new gas grill.

"The options are overwhelming, Sophie," he said. "I don't know what we'd all do without *Consumer Reports*."

Rosie was a pretty woman with naturally wavy long blond hair. It was lovely just hanging down over her shoulders, but she usually wore it pinned up in a bun. She was very skinny, used no make-up and wore thick glasses.

Mark had brown hair like me, but he was as skinny as Rosie. I was the only one in my family with any meat on my bones. He wore thick glasses too. In fact he and Rosie looked a lot alike.

They arrived this morning wearing matching flannel shirts. Rosie gave me a can of salt-free peanuts and a bag of cashews with so much salt you could see it in little clumps at the bottom of the bag.

"What's a yin without a little yang now and then?" she said.

After Mark read the ingredients on my orange juice carton, he helped himself to a glass and sat down. I put my favorite tacky plastic placemats on the wooden table. On each was a picture of a red lobster standing on its flippers with a big toothy smile and an American flag in one claw. I had no idea where Robin or Dan could be. I asked Mark what was new.

"Well, we're upgrading our microwave to a —"

"Oh Mark," Rosie said. "I hope there are other things that are new in our lives besides the microwave." She picked up a rolled up napkin, unraveled it and rolled it up again. Their communication lines looked like they needed to be tethered a bit tighter.

"What's wrong, Sophie?" he said. "You look tired."

"I am."

"You're sick, aren't you?"

"Yeah, I've got Seasonal Life Sucks Disorder. I'll be fine in the spring."

He looked hurt. My sarcasm wasn't called for. "I'm sorry," I said. "I'm just going through some rough times."

Mark looked the lox over carefully. I didn't know what he was looking for and thought it would ruin my appetite if I asked. The phone rang once. Robin must have gotten it upstairs.

"What kind of rough times?" Mark asked.

"Oh, just some trouble at work. I'll be okay."

That answer satisfied him, for now.

"Do you know the mercury content of this?" Mark pointed to the lox.

"No, Mark," I said.

"It's more than the fillings in your teeth."

"What does mercury do to you?" I asked, bonehead that I am.

"Mercury may well be a causative factor in arthritis, and may also contribute to depression and confusion. You should watch it."

Rosie was laughing, but after a minute she picked the lox off her bagel and put it on the side of her plate. I took it off her plate and put it on top of my already loxed bagel.

"Mom," Robin called, "it's the detective."

Oh, Christ. How was I going to explain this?

I ran upstairs and scooted my daughter out of the bedroom.

"Hello," I said into the receiver. "Wait a minute. Who is this?"

"Samms." It sounded like him. Pretty soon, I'm going to think my rooms are bugged.

"Well, what is it?" I said.

"Looks like a man in a dark blue van bought the sea worms."

"And?" I said.

"We found the bait shop, but they couldn't identify him other than to say that he was middle aged and had dark hair. Of course, the description means nothing," he said. "Anybody could disguise themselves. But the van is important. Do you know anybody who drives a dark blue van?"

"Could it have been a pick-up truck?"

"No, they were sure."

"Then I can't help you." I went to the window and slowly pushed the lace curtain aside. Now the fog was so dense I couldn't even see the grape arbor. "There's something I've been meaning to discuss with you," I said.

"Yes?"

I went to the bed and plopped down.

"Why did you decide that Eliot Wohlman would be your professional consultant and not a suspect? I told you about my suspicions."

"He *is* a suspect."

"That's not how he sees it. He thinks he's going to help you."

"Look, I'm not going to tell him he's a suspect if I can get more out of him by letting him think I need his expertise."

"Oh."

"Anything else?"

"I bet you're going to tell me to leave the detective work to you."

"I'm not going to waste my breath," he said, but he was laughing. After we hung up, I went downstairs to the kitchen.

"What was that about?" Mark asked.

"I can't really say. It involves a patient."

Dan had joined the gathering while I was gone. We were still angry at each other but had toned it down for now.

"If you're having problems, Sophie, we're here to help you day or night," Mark said.

I touched his hand. "I know you are."

We were all discussing garbage disposals when Robin came in. Her stripes were horizontal.

"Hi, cutie," I said. "What have you been doing?"

"Nothing, Mom," she said. I gave everyone my "you ought to take notes on effective parenting" smile. "What did the detective say?" she asked.

"Not much, Robin. Everything's okay."

She looked at me with doubt on her face and it broke my heart.

She went to the refrigerator and opened the door. We watched as she closed the door and tried the freezer. As she stared at the ground turkey, my brother said, "Sophie, you should consider frost-free."

"What?"

"A frost-free freezer. A freezer that has frost in it runs at a less efficient level than a —"

"Mark." Rosie grabbed his arm. "Enough."

Robin left her post at the fridge, and gave them each a kiss before grabbing her jacket and running out the back door. I didn't know what she intended to do in the foggy yard. I guess she just wanted to be alone.

I picked up a second bagel and slathered it with cream cheese.

"Did she have breakfast?" asked Rosie.

"I doubt it," I said.

Dan knew my discomfort. Even though we were still fighting he tried to help me. "I think the reason she's a picky eater is to drive her mother crazy," he offered.

"And does it?" Rosie asked.

"Not at all." I wrapped the remaining slice of lox around my finger and sucked it off.

It took until Monday morning for me to cool off in my fury towards Dan, but I wasn't ready to give it up entirely. I could beat anybody in a grudge marathon.

A continuous heavy drizzle made it sound like troops of soldiers were marching in the distance. It never seemed to stop raining on the Cape in February. I was at the office by ten. I had on my Monday morning, having eaten too much over the weekend, full bodied black shift. I couldn't hear Gracie in the waiting room. I checked it out to find no one there. Ten minutes later, I heard the door.

Gracie came running in, giving me a big smile and wearing jeans and a heavy tan vee neck sweater.

"Sorry I'm late." She took the chair closest to the door.

In every office I've had, patients sat in the chair nearest the exit. A subconscious assurance of being close to an escape.

"Your detective came to my house this morning," she said.

I wished she didn't call him my detective.

"He asked me all these questions about where I was at different times. I think he thinks I'm the one who's been threatening you."

"No, no Gracie. He's asking lots of people. It's not just you."

"Well, that's a relief. But I'm really sorry about what you're going through. You must be scared to death."

"Every psychiatrist deals with this. I'm okay. Do you feel shaken up by anything the detective said?"

"No. He was only there about five minutes. Then there was a tie up on Route 28. So I'm really sorry I'm late."

She was obviously a good actress. I was sure that Samms would have brought up the arrest to her. I knew I had to...one way or another.

"Gracie, there's something we need to discuss."

"Sure." No look of concern on her face at all.

"Detective Samms is naturally concerned that one of my patients might be behind the threats I've been getting, so he's particularly interested in people who have been arrested. I wouldn't give him this information, of course, but he could easily find it out himself."

"Okay. What did you want to discuss?"

And I thought this would be easy.

"Have you ever been arrested, Gracie?"

"No, of course not."

She didn't want to tell me about it. Fine. Patients don't have to tell their therapists what they don't want them to know. I looked out at the harbor. The tide was full moon low. I could see the *Pilgrim* across the way. There was a light in the little cabin and I could barely make out the captain and his dog. He appeared to be bent over a table, looking at charts or something like that. The husky was beside him, seemingly looking at the charts too. The lit cabin was a warm sight on the cold colorless harbor.

Gracie's emotional life continued on a crash course. Last week's declarations seemed to have washed out to sea. Halfway through her hour, she mentioned a budding concern.

"He thinks...you're going to tell someone he's seeing me," she said, "and he also thinks you'll try to talk me out of seeing him anymore."

"Gracie, I would not tell anyone you're seeing him."

This direction was making me nervous. I tried to sort out what was objective and what wasn't.

She rested her elbow on the arm of the wingback and tilted her head so she could twirl her gray hair around her finger. "Lately he's been getting jealous of everything. I used to feel good that he was this way, like it proved how much he loved me." She shifted arms and twirled a strand on the other side. "But now it's beginning to get to me. It bothers him when I talk to anybody, anybody at all. He thinks I'm talking about him. Every time I ask him to calm down and give me some space, it just makes him angry." She laughed a nervous laugh. I remained serious.

"I'm scared," she said. "He's not acting like the person I used to know."

I felt the pricklies all over.

"And there's one more thing."

I wasn't sure I wanted to hear this.

"He's been stalking me. I see him in his car parked down the block. I mean five hours later, in the middle of the night, he's still there."

"Don't you think you should tell the police?" I asked.

"No! Of course not. He'd be furious. I'd never see him again."

That was the main issue.

"You're the person he's worried about the most," she said. "He says if you tell anyone about him, he could be kicked off the hospital staff. I told him you would never say anything, but he said all counselors talk about their patients, especially to other counselors."

I thought I heard the waiting room door open.

I felt a small pain in the center of my chest, which happens when I'm very tense. Trying to relax my shoulders and breathe out fully, I said, "Has he ever followed you after you've left your house?"

She was back to twirling. "Well, yes, yesterday. He followed me all the way from my house to my dance class, but he said he was just making sure I was safe because of icy roads, not that I believed him. I bet he follows me all the time."

The captain and his dog were now on the side of the boat. They jumped off the boat and onto the pier. The boards were rain-soaked and probably slippery, but both of them were sure-footed as they walked down the pier. I tuned back to Gracie. "Do you feel angry that he follows you?"

"Sometimes yes and sometimes no. Part of me feels good that he cares that much. I just wish he wasn't so sneaky about it."

"Have you told him that?"

"No way."

"Do you think he's going to leave his wife to be with you someday?"

She stood up from the chair and straightened out her sweater as if it had been pulling in the back. "If he really wanted to stay in his marriage, why would he take the chance of seeing me?" she asked.

"Maybe he wants his marriage and he wants you too."

She went to the pendulum and touched it. She appeared mesmerized for a moment by the slow movement of the circles it formed.

She sat back down. "But he can't have both," she said.

"Actually, he seems to have both now, don't you think?"

So needy. I hated to watch women like this stay in never-never land. If Eliot left his family, chances are Gracie would lose interest in him, because she wasn't ready for a commitment. She hadn't dealt with the underlying problems, which were her family issues, of course.

"I know you think I'm looking for my father in him." She put her hand, palm out, toward me in a stop position. I always heeded that warning. "My dad wasn't anything like Eliot. Dad was never there for me. He wouldn't even say 'hello' to me when he came in the front door."

Ultimately, Eliot wasn't there for her either. Or that other doctor for that matter. I used to see his wife at hospital functions too.

"What was that like for you?" I said.

"It was awful." She retrieved some old tissues from her purse and began to cry.

The waiting room door opened and closed. This time I was sure of it.

"I was just a little girl," she said between sniffles, "and I never asked for much. In fact, I never asked for anything. I can picture myself looking out the window next to the front door and waiting for his car to pull in. When I'd see it, I'd run to the door and open it. But he'd just walk past me and pat me on my head. That was all I got…a pat on the head. He wouldn't even say hello. Just one lousy pat on the head."

"Did you feel you deserved that?"

"I don't know." Most girls forgave their fathers, but few forgave their mothers.

"What was your mother like?"

"Oh, she wasn't as bad, I guess, but we weren't real close either." She bent her head to curl a strand of hair around her finger and looked out at the harbor. We watched the captain and his dog turn the corner and go behind the big old empty building that used to be an ice-making plant. It was probably in its heyday during the time fishermen in my building were packing tuna.

Gracie said, "I always felt like I was in her way."

"How so?"

She stopped playing with her hair. "Well, now that you brought it up, I remember one Saturday night when she was having a dinner party. I must have been around eight or nine. I couldn't wait because I was invited too, and I had been looking forward to dressing up and seeing my mother's best china and tablecloth. I remember these tiny silver dishes next to each plate, barely an inch long, that she put salt in, and next to them she put tiny silver spoons." She was wide-eyed as she pictured the magical setting.

"My mother wore a red Chinese silk dress. Yes…I can just picture it. And she had on black beaded pumps. I said, 'Oh Mommy, you are the most beautiful thing I ever saw. Why, you're a vision.'"

Gracie tried to control her emotions and continued to talk. "I remember I was hoping I could help fix the table so that maybe when everybody said how gorgeous everything was, I could feel proud that it was partly my doing. Mom said something like, 'Gracie, if you'll go sit in the den like a good girl while I do a few things around here, then I promise I'll come get you and give you something to do.' Well," she sniffed, "I guess the rest of the story's pretty predictable. I sat by myself in the den waiting for my mother. She forgot to come get me." She looked down and picked at her nail polish.

She thought for a moment and looked back up at me. "That's a really stupid story, isn't it?"

Gracie's attention was focused on her mother, but her father didn't sound like any great shakes either.

"Gracie," I said, "those are important stories and I can see that the feelings are just as alive today."

We didn't speak for a while. We looked out the window. The swells were growing larger with the now incoming tide. The *Pilgrim* rocked hypnotically on the sea. Gracie watched it, lost in her reverie.

Then she continued, "But it wasn't like they beat me or anything."

"I know, but sometimes the kind of emotional detachment you describe can be just as devastating as physical abuse."

We stayed silent for a few minutes, watching the swells.

I began again, "Your parents weren't bad people. They probably didn't know the impact their actions had on you. But you don't deserve to be ignored, Gracie. Nobody does."

After another minute, I asked her about her present involvement with her mother. Her father had died several years ago.

"Well, I don't see her much. She lives in Connecticut and she's pretty occupied with her new husband. They travel a lot."

There's a tendency to defend parents, no matter what.

"When did you speak with her last?"

She picked at her nail polish some more. "I didn't really speak with her. I sent her a Christmas card."

"And did she respond?"

"She's very busy."

I heard the clock chime six times. She looked relieved. "Doctor

Green?" She stood up to leave. "I want to thank you. I am feeling better." Her eyes watered and she added, "I mean it." It looked like she had much more to say.

"So long, Gracie." I knew I had been of little help.

"Goodbye, Doctor Green." She gave me a tentative wave and left. So fragile.

I listened for sounds in the waiting room even though the door had opened twice, indicating someone had come and gone. Paranoia set in. I peered out my office door, then walked around the waiting room, looking under the couch and behind everything. No one was there.

Back at my desk, I made a few notes in Gracie's file. Digging through my drawer, the only thing I could find was a half eaten Nestlé's Crunch and a relish packet from Burger King. Now, I thought that the chocolate was in the simple carbohydrate category because it's made with sugar. The relish was definitely a complex carb because it was made from a cucumber. Therefore, since the veggie carbs are so much better for you, the nasty simple carbs would be cancelled out by slathering them with relish.

The rest of the day sped by quickly. My last patient was through at five thirty.

I put on my tweed coat and got my briefcase. I was edgy, knowing that there was no one else in the building. I should have let Dan meet me in the waiting room at night, but this morning I hadn't felt like being cooperative. On the other hand, being independent was one thing; being stupid was another. I left the suite and closed the waiting room door. I was just about to lock it.

Across the hall, the door to a vacant office was open. It was black inside. When I was a child, I had to go past my brother's bedroom door in the middle of the night if I needed the bathroom. He used to hear me get out of bed and would wait by his dark door. When I walked by, he'd jump out and scream bloody murder. It used to scare the hell out of me. To this day, I can't look into a dark doorway without expecting somebody to jump out of it.

A clunk came from the empty office.

I froze.

I couldn't look in the doorway.

Move, Sophie. Force yourself, damn it! But my hands were shaking too much to get the key in the door lock.

Forget about it. Just get out of here!

I slowly turned around and looked in the door.

Nothing.

I couldn't see into the room. I was too frightened to reach in and find a light switch.

Just go down the stairs, one at a time, Sophie. Breathe deeply.

If I took it slow, I'd be all right. If I started to get hysterical, panic would take over, and I would feel compelled to race down the stairs.

One step. That's right.

Now another step.

CLUNK.

I tore down the stairs, terrified, and tripped on the last two. My forehead hit the facing wall.

CLUNK.

Reeling with fright, I quickly snatched up my briefcase from the floor and raced out of the building into the dark drizzly night.

I looked frantically for the Blazer. I ran when I saw it.

"Dan!" I said, panting. "There's someone in that empty office!" Still I couldn't breathe. "And the lights are off!" I pointed to the window you could see from the parking lot, the kind of window that you unlatch from the side. It was open. It slammed shut and opened again on its hinges.

"The wind." He got out of the truck to hold me from collapse. "That's the noise you heard. It made the window close."

"How can you be sure?" I looked up at him, still panting.

"I've been watching it blow open and closed while I've been here. Come with me." He took my hand. "We'll go and close it together."

"Up there?"

He nodded. We went back into the building and upstairs. He reached in the room and felt for the overhead light switch. A hand poked out and grabbed his arm.

"Dan!" I screamed.

Someone pulled him into the room.

I ran into the darkness. I could make out Dan on the floor with a man on top of him. I smashed my briefcase into the man's back. He groaned and Dan got up. He grabbed the guy by the collar, but he broke free. I found the light switch and flipped it up. The man had on a mask but it was unmistakably Carl Darby.

"Carl, leave us alone!" I screamed. He turned to bolt, but Dan got hold of his coat from behind.

"I'm not letting you leave here. Get the police, Sophie."

I didn't want to leave him alone with Carl. I hesitated and Dan shouted, "Get the police!" But Carl took that moment to yank himself away from Dan's hold and run down the stairs.

"Are you okay?" I held my husband for dear life.

"Yes." He put his arms around me.

"Will we ever feel safe again?" I asked.

He didn't answer.

We went back to my office and told Samms by phone what happened. He said he'd send a car to the area, but that so far Carl had eluded the police every time they thought they had him.

Dan and I walked down the stairs. We sat on the bottom step to catch our breath.

"Did he hurt you?" I said.

"No." He put his head in his hands. "He didn't hit me — just pushed me down."

"I never knew I could act like that," I said. "I just whammed him with my briefcase without thinking twice."

"That was smart." He put his hand on my knee.

We stayed silent for a while, still trying to catch our breath and process the ordeal.

"I wonder what I would have done if I had a gun," I said. "I mean it was all so fast. It was weird."

"You acted on instinct. We're programmed to do that."

"And I've never seen you so aggressive. Were you scared?"

"Of course."

In a few minutes we calmed down.

"My hero." I swooned, putting my head on his shoulder and looking up at him.

"Now you like me."

"Yep."

"I thought you weren't impressed with my machismo."

"Well I am now. You're the manliest man this side of Kalamazoo."

I took his hand and pulled him up. We left the building. Without even asking the other, we turned away from the truck and walked out of the parking lot and onto the beach. It was still drizzling, but we didn't care.

"I'm sorry, Dan."

He was silent.

"I'm not sorry about being furious at you. I'm sorry about the way I talked to you."

"I appreciate you saying that." We held hands and walked along the dark shore. The sand dunes were dark silhouettes behind the tall blowing reeds. On the other side of the harbor, in the direction of Hyannis, the sky was brighter. I thought about Carl and how isolated we were out here and I suggested we head back to the truck.

"Don't you want to say something to me?" I asked.

"Not really."

"You don't?"

"I don't."

"Don't you want to say, 'My darling, Sophie. I'm sorry too. I'm sorry I went against your wishes and I promise never to do it again.' And then you want to add, 'And I forgive you for the nasty things you said about me. I know you were just upset and you didn't mean any of it, except the part about going behind your back. That part you meant.' Go ahead, Dan. I'm ready."

He laughed out loud, but he never did say any of it.

On the ride home, I smelled the indescribable odor of Chinese food. I turned around. Behind the front seat were two big bags full of the stuff.

"Ooooh!"

"I need a truce tonight," he said. He held my hand tenderly. "Let's have this night be a good one."

"I would love that, sweetheart."

At home, I changed into my sweats. We spread the Chinese food boxes all over the kitchen table. Robin looked like she was drooling. I got some silverware but Dan had chopsticks for himself.

There were egg rolls, chicken fingers, spareribs with the bone in, fried rice with pork, pork strips, and beef chow mein.

Yowie zowie.

"At last, some decent food around this house," Robin said.

"But this food is tainted with MSG and laced with sugary duck sauce," I said, placing an entire chicken finger in my mouth. Dan was working on the chopsticks. Five grains of rice almost made it to his mouth before landing on his sleeve. Robin and I tried not to laugh.

Dan tabled his unhappiness for this lovely, though brief time. He tried again with the chopsticks. "Food tastes better when it's eaten in the authentic way," he said. I figured it would take him five more tries before he would grab a fork.

Robin took some chow mein and two spare ribs. If she reached for the last one, I vowed that I would control my impulse to rap her knuckles with my fork. I looked over at Dan who was trying to balance a water chestnut between his chopsticks. He had found that if he put his face practically on the plate, he could just about toss the food in. The water chestnut missed the mouth and landed on the floor. We pretended not to notice. I could see his hand slowly inching toward the fork.

"So tell me what's new, Robin." She and I were trying so hard to control ourselves.

Dan grabbed the fork and shoveled in the chow mein like a starving coal miner off a three year strike.

Robin volunteered to do the dishes, which added up to just the forks since the paper plates went into the garbage. The only leftover for the fridge was the box of fried rice.

My stomach was stretched beyond natural proportions. I groaned my way to the couch.

The phone rang and I heard my mother's voice on the answering machine, which was attached to the phone in the kitchen. I was too immobilized to move. "Are you going to pick it up?" Dan asked.

"I'll call her back later, when I've recovered," I said.

He turned on the tube which we normally wheel in front of the couch. We put our feet on the old brown chest we use as a coffee table.

I began my usual self-imposed guilt trip.

I'll call her back in an hour. But what if, between now and then, she falls down the steps and has a heart attack and dies?

Sophie, I continued to myself, act like an adult and watch TV. Later, you'll feel more like talking and you will, so don't give in to guilt.

I picked up the phone next to the couch and dialed her number.

On the first ring, I told myself that it was time I stopped lying to my mother. I'm a psychiatrist, for heaven's sake. I would tell her the truth about not answering the phone.

"Hi Ma, it's me. How are you?"

"Where were you, Sophie? I called two minutes ago."

"I was in the bathroom."

I took off my left sock and tried to find a pressure point on the bottom of my foot, one that might make me mature in eleven seconds.

"Well…what did you have for dinner?" she asked.

"We gorged on Chinese food. I can hardly breathe."

"With all that salt, yet?"

"That is correct."

"MSG is just plain salt those people disguise with a fancy name. And let me tell you, they put it in everything. When you ask them to cook you a dish without MSG, first they pretend they don't understand you, then they nod 'yes', and then they go back in the kitchen and have a good laugh."

"Mo-ther!"

"I hope you didn't have their pork. They never cook it enough. That's why you get it so fast. You ever see one of them eating the pork? Of course not. That's because they know what's going on and just stick with the rice."

In my well-adjusted voice I said, "No, Ma. We didn't eat any pork."

Cover mouthpiece and sigh, twice.

"Well, I've got a gigantic day tomorrow. I should hit the sack."

"But I haven't had a chance to talk about why I called."

"What is it?"

"You're too tired I guess."

"I'm not. Please Ma."

"I just wanted to talk to you for a minute, make sure you're all right."

"Of course I'm all right."

"If it's some kind of illness, I want to know." Her voice broke as she said this. "We have enough money and you…could see our doctor."

"I'm not sick. I don't want you to worry about me."

"I'm afraid that something's going to happen to you." We never talked about Jeremy. It was still too painful, even after all these years. Although she couldn't say his name, she still talked about him metaphorically in the way she was doing now. Always worried that some horrible fate would befall me the way it did her son. She continued, "I'm afraid that if something happened to you I won't get a chance to say…"

"Say what?" I asked softly.

A long hesitation, and then she said, "Oh Sophie, your father's calling."

"He can wait, mamala. Tell me what you want to say."

There was silence. And then she sighed. "It's nothing, Sophie. I'll talk to you tomorrow." We both hung up longing to connect in a way we hadn't. Why was it so damned hard to have an intimate talk with my mother? I was too old to let any moments of closeness pass me by.

My body was transported to the kitchen where the fried rice was waiting.

"Sophie," Dan called from the living room, "what are you doing?"

"Nufring." A few rice pieces escaped my mouth. I was picking them up from the floor when he came in. "Just cleaning up," I said.

He knelt beside me and took the rice box away. I grabbed it back. "Rice is good for the intestines," I said. "You know the BRAT diet. Bagels, rice, apricot preserves and tacos. That's what doctors say to eat when you're sick." He wrenched the box away.

"I always think of you as sick, but I don't think rice will help."

"Very funny."

"Ten minutes ago, you were complaining about feeling miserable. You're going to feel worse if you eat any more." He put the box away. It was most courageous of him to talk to me about overeating.

"How about we go to bed?" he said. "We're not going to worry about anything tonight." He put his hands on my shoulders.

"Dan," I said, "you're the best thing since Grandma's kreplach."

The phone rang and we both jumped.

It was a tracer call from my answering service. There was a message from Hyannis Hospital. A Doctor Corbut wanted to talk with me regarding an admission. Her name was Gracie Brill.

Chapter Eight

Monday, 10:15 PM

The person on the desk at the hospital put me right through.

"Doctor Corbut here."

"Yes, Phil. It's Sophie Green. You admitted Gracie Brill?"

"I'm glad you called, Sophie." He sounded relieved. "Gracie's been here about a half hour. She slashed both wrists, but thankfully, she didn't do a good job of it."

"How did she get to the hospital?" I asked. I couldn't believe it.

"She must have changed her mind because she called the rescue squad. She was hysterical when they picked her up. When I saw her in the ER, she asked for you, said she had just seen you. The problem is, her physical status is fine, but I hate to discharge her tomorrow. I can't do a mental status. She's non-talkative. I figured you could help. Do you think you could make it tonight? I know you're not on call, but..."

"I'll be there in forty-five minutes. Are you on the third floor?"

"Yes. Have me paged when you get here."

I wouldn't let Dan take me to the hospital. It was late and he was exhausted after the harrowing ordeal with Carl at the office. When I arrived, Phil met me at the nurses' station.

"Sophie. Good to see you." He shook my hand. We had seen each other at a few medical staff meetings but hadn't spoken much. He was a very pleasant looking guy, fair haired, about forty-five. Either he had trouble with contact lenses or he had a nervous eye twitch.

Gracie had signed a release that made it all right for me to discuss her history with him, although in an emergency I could have done it anyway.

"Frankly, Phil, I'm surprised she did this. I'll check back with you after I've seen her."

Gracie was lying in bed watching TV. Her wrists were bandaged. I tried not to think of my exhaustion.

"Doctor Green!" she said. "Wait a minute. I'll turn this off." She fidgeted with the remote control until the television was off. I sat on the bed alongside her. She put her head back on the pillow and allowed tears to run down her cheeks.

"I'm sor…"

"No, Gracie," I said. "You don't need to apologize to me."

"Well," she sniffed, "I let you down. I know I did."

"What happened?"

She sighed. "After our appointment, I felt terrible. There was something I hadn't told you, and I should have." She sat up. "So I went straight home and got upset with myself…for a lot of reasons. I'm screwing up my life. What the hell am I doing?" She stopped talking. I could hear a muffled voice on the intercom in the hallway.

"You were trying to make the pain go away," I said.

"Is that what this looks like?" She held up her wrists.

"Well, actually it does. I'd like to hear what happened right before you did this to yourself."

"Well…" She twirled a lock of her hair. It looked pathetic with the bandages on her wrist. "There were three messages on my answering machine. All of them were from Eliot. The first one was fine, he was just calling to say hello. The second one was odd. He was upset that I wasn't home, and said he needed to see me." She grabbed a few tissues and blew her nose. "You see, after our session, I made a decision to break it off with Eliot. I mean, the relationship is bad for me. The man is married, for God's sake."

"You don't have to make quick decisions on these things," I said.

"I know, I know. I just felt that if I didn't do it now, then I never would." I was beginning to get the picture. "Well, the third message was that I had better be home in one hour, and that's exactly when my doorbell rang." She was talking faster now.

"When I let him in, he took me in his arms and kissed me. Then we sat on the couch. I felt afraid of him. I've been afraid for some time now." She looked at me. "He said he had some big news. It was what I've been wanting to hear since I met him. He said he was going to leave his wife." She was crying loudly now, and I was sure she could be heard in the hallway but I didn't want to stop her. Between sobs, she said, "I...didn't...want him to. I panicked."

I put my arms around her and let her cry. We rocked together. At this moment, I felt closer to Gracie than I did with my own daughter.

She sat back and continued to keep her arms on my shoulders. "It was awful. I pretended to be happy, and he had to leave anyway so I only had to pretend for a few minutes, but when he left I fell apart." She broke her hold on me and reached for more tissues. Thank goodness the hospital staff knew to stay out of this.

"I felt so hopeless," she said, "and the feeling was unbearable. Nothing was right, nothing. Not Eliot, not my mother, not my father." She held her breath for a long time. "And nothing was ever going to be right."

"So you decided suicide was the only option?"

"Yes." She started to get out of bed but then stopped herself. "There's something else," she said.

"Go ahead. You can tell me."

"I've...well, I've tried to do this before."

I waited. She hesitated, obviously uncomfortable.

"Gracie," I said, "I'm glad you trust me enough to talk about this, and I'm not angry at you. There's always a right time to tell someone these things, and it just hasn't been the right time for you yet. That's okay."

It was a bad idea for Gracie to dredge up emotions about a previous suicide attempt. That would only intensify her present feelings. But on the other hand, if she had to, she had to.

"Well, I'd rather not talk about it now," she said. "I just felt I was betraying you by keeping it a secret."

"You weren't betraying me. You decide what you want to bring up in therapy, or anywhere else for that matter." I took both of her hands in mine. "What did you think you'd gain by killing yourself today?" I said.

"I thought I wouldn't have to deal with Eliot or any of the agony anymore."

"There are other ways."

"But I'm not strong enough."

"Someday you'll think so. Someday you'll recognize the strength and courage I know is in you."

She looked up at me with that wide-eyed hope. We were still

holding hands.

"Why didn't you call me?" I said.

"Oh I couldn't do that."

"Of course you could."

She looked out the window. "I haven't been honest with you. I didn't tell you about my other suicide attempt, and some other stuff," she said. "I couldn't call you. I'd feel like I was bothering you."

"Have I ever acted that way?"

"Well, no." She held on to my hands. "I just assumed…"

"Why not test some of these assumptions about other people?"

"What if I'm right?" -

"What if you're wrong?"

"How do I start?"

"You already did. You tested your assumption with me."

I stood up and looked out the window at the parking lot. I hate hospitals, the same way everybody else does.

Gracie needed something concrete to do. "I'd like you to begin a game plan for yourself," I said. "There's plenty of life ahead for you, with good times and bad times, and you're not going to miss it." She looked at me with trust in her eyes. "I'd like you to write down on a piece of paper one step you're going to take. I don't care how small it is, just make it something positive you're going to do for yourself. I want to see something in writing when I come back tomorrow. Do I have your word?"

She nodded.

"I've got to go now, but I'll be back tomorrow."

Phil was at the nurses' station flirting with a pretty brunette. His eye tic seemed worse.

"Phil…" I waved and got his attention. He pulled himself away.

"What do you think?" he said.

"I think she'll be okay, but I'd like her to stay here at least two more days. My feeling is that it was an unpremeditated impulsive act. There's no major depression or persistent ideation. I'll be back tomorrow."

I walked to the elevator and pushed the button. Finally I could go home and collapse. The door slid open and Eliot Wohlman stepped out.

"How is she?" he said.

"Eliot, you know I can't discuss a patient."

"Tell me how she is, or I'll pull the records myself."

"Go right ahead."

His ruddy face became like stone. "You shouldn't be talking to me like this," he said.

"I've had enough of you," I said. "You're a disgrace to the profession. And you're an impediment to Gracie's mental well being."

"Don't you think she should be the one to tell me, or do you do all of your patients' important work for them?"

"How did you know she was in here anyhow?"

"She called *me* for help." He laughed as he entered her room.

Chapter Nine

Tuesday, 2 PM

Brilliant sunlight sparkled off the small crests of the waves. The sands were no longer gray but the color of coffee with cream. On this rare clear February day, the colors of the Cape — the royal ocean blues, the stands of reeds in golds — emerged like a starburst.

Charlie came into my office. His suit looked wrinkled and his tie was askew.

"Detective Samms came to my house," he said.

"I'm so sorry about that, Charlie. I've been having some trouble with somebody threatening me and he wanted to question my patients. I never meant for him to do this."

"Well, he was very nice, but I don't understand why I was questioned."

"Everyone I see was," I lied.

"You sound like you're in a lot of danger," he said.

This was one of the things I hated about Samms talking to my patients. Nobody should be in therapy and worrying about their therapist.

I sat up and looked directly at him. "I want to tell you something very important, Charlie. I know that there was no reason whatsoever for that detective to question you. You have nothing to do with what's been going on. I tried to talk him out of questioning everyone but I couldn't." That seemed to make him feel better. "Let's not talk about me, Charlie. Tell me about you."

"I, uh...I'm..." He was about to bring up his mother, but then I saw a change-of-mind in his expression. "I don't know if I've ever told you how bad it gets."

"How bad what gets?"

"My OCD. That's what you call it, right?"

"Yes. Would you like to tell me about it now?"

"Oh very much. I need to get this out." His expression turned to one of relief. That's what symptoms do. They take people away from the problem. "I'm always checking things over and over again, even though I know I've already done them. Like the oven, for example. I have to run my finger around the dials to make sure they're really on the OFF position. And the coffee pot, I have to touch the empty plug with my fingers even though I can see that there's no plug in it."

It's amazing how much I'm like so many of my patients. I think everybody's crazy to a certain degree. It's a matter of how much it impairs our lives. It's also a matter of how good we are at hiding it, from ourselves as well as others. But now wasn't the right time to examine my own quirks. And hopefully that time wouldn't present itself anywhere in the near future.

Charlie continued to talk about his symptoms rather than his grief. "I have to check the plug at least seven times. Then I go to the back slider. I can see that the lock is down but I have to touch it again and again to make sure. Then I start over again. I get up at four in the morning because it takes me two hours and twenty-four minutes to get myself together before I can work at the computer. I can barely go to sleep because I worry that the alarm isn't set, even though I haven't changed the wake-up time in years. I get up eight or ten times just to make sure it's set for four AM."

He took a tissue and dried his already dried forehead. It was starting to get red. I felt such compassion for this kind and pathetic man. The fact that he wasn't talking about his mother was so much like him — focusing on his compulsive acts in an attempt to control the uncontrollable. Of course, as life presented more uncontrollable realities, his symptoms got far worse. He looked at me for approval to go on and I gave him a nod.

"Sometimes it gets even more ridiculous. I really hate myself, honest to God, for the things I have to do. When I'm driving, I actually have to take my wallet out of my back pocket and take my license out to be sure I have it with me even though I checked that before I left the house. Most of these things require eleven times of checking. Ten is a good number. But eleven is, too. Anything that doesn't have a six in it is safe." He stopped for a moment — I think to make sure I wasn't going to tell him that what he was thinking was preposterous. "I'm afraid that if I don't check it out that one more time, then I could be wrong. And if I'm wrong, the house could burn down or some other horrible thing could happen. Or…" He stopped talking.

"Or what, Charlie?" Here I go again. It was getting a little more difficult for me to be certain that he wasn't my enemy.

"Or…I might do something to someone I care about."

I couldn't think of anyone he had mentioned that he cared about other than me and his mother. This was just too much.

"Who are you talking about?" I had to ask the question. It was for my own benefit, but I had to.

"I'm talking about — I'm talking about —" He started to wipe his forehead again but stopped himself. By now the tissue was too dirty for him and he had to get another. This action calmed him. As usual, the compulsive act took his mind away from reality. God only knows what would happen if he ever made himself control the cleanliness compulsions.

"I don't know who I was talking about."

We both sighed together.

"It sounds like torture, Charlie."

"I don't want to take any pills for this, Doctor Green. I swear I don't. That would make me feel even more out of control."

"I know that you feel this way about medicine."

"I suppose you think I'm nuts," he said.

"No Charlie, I don't. I just think you are extremely troubled by your behavior."

"I am."

It was crazy for me not to mention his mother's death, but I had to be careful. "How are you doing about your mom?" I said as quietly as I could.

He looked at my table in front of the window and saw a clump of dust on it. He carefully removed it with another tissue. "I'm very unhappy, Doctor Green. I'm very, very sad. I go to sleep every night expecting to see Mom in the morning. And every day I get up and she's not there, I feel like I'm re-living the shock all over again."

"I think it will be like that for a while," I said.

He gave me the oddest look at that point, sort of like adoration or love. Or at least the kind of look he'd have on his face if he wanted to tell me he loved me. I wouldn't be surprised if he believed he was in love with me. Not only was I the one person that he could talk to about his OCD, I was also now a mother replacement.

"Was there something you wanted to say?" I asked.

"I wish you were..." And then he stopped as our time was up.

After he left I tried to fill in the blanks. Who did he wish I was? His mother? His wife?

I looked out the window at the sea. A few mergansers were diving for fish. One lone eider was probably wondering where the rest of his pals were. The *Pilgrim* was gone, and glittering ice was mounding on the pilings where it was usually docked.

After two more patients, I closed up shop. When I left the building, I noticed an officer in a police car. It was way at the end of the parking lot, behind a small stand of pitch pine. The policeman was pleasant when I introduced myself. Evidently he was familiar with what was going on, and said Samms had asked him to keep an eye on the place.

"I don't want everybody questioned who's just walking into the building."

"I know that. The detective explained your case to us."

"I'm just not sure he knows what he's doing. My problem is touchy. You can't just bulldoze your way in like you can with simpler problems."

"Believe me, no problems that Detective Samms deals with are simple. He takes the hard ones." He laughed in a nice way. "Samms has commendations from every precinct he's worked in. And he keeps them stuffed in some drawer, not on the precinct wall." That sounded like me and my diplomas.

"May I ask you something? I keep noticing a limp and a knee problem. What's wrong with him?"

He shook his head. "I don't know. I've asked him that myself, but he just laughs it off and says it's an old injury. I have the feeling that there's a story there, but nobody's ever heard it."

I thanked him for being there and drove to the hospital to see Gracie.

Chapter Ten

Tuesday, 5:30 PM

Phil Corbut left a brief note in Gracie's file indicating that she was stabilized for the last twenty-four hours and pending my approval, she could be discharged at any time. That would mean one day shorter than I'm usually comfortable with, but I would think about it.

I could hear loud voices coming from her room.

"It's over, Eliot, so you might as well leave now," I heard Gracie say.

I knocked on the door and pushed it open. They were standing at the foot of the bed. Eliot glanced at me, then took her bandaged hand in his.

"You're in a crisis, Gracie. Doctor Green would agree with me that this isn't a good time to make decisions." He looked at me. "You know I'm right. Please tell her that."

"You needed a crisis to make this decision, Gracie," I said. "Don't let anyone talk you out of it."

He stared at me with fury in his eyes.

"Doctor Wohlman, I would like to speak with Gracie alone, please."

Like two dogs in a dominance competition, our eyes were fixed on each other. I was not going to look away first.

"I'm going nowhere," he said angrily. "She needs to be protected from you. You almost let her die."

Don't listen.

"You'll have to leave now, Eliot," I said, "or I'm calling security."

She looked pleadingly up at him.

I went to the patient call button and pressed it. "In less than a minute a nurse will be here, Eliot. I'll be glad to explain all of this."

He grabbed his keys and strode past me, not saying a word to either of us. Gracie and I exhaled audibly.

She went to her night table and picked up a piece of paper. "Now I bet you can guess what I wrote down I would do."

"End your relationship. What a decision." I wouldn't ask her if she was sure about it, because I knew she'd never be.

We sat on the bed.

"He can be pretty scary," she said.

"Apparently."

"I'm through with him, Doctor Green."

She looked like she meant it.

"And guess what else?" she said. "I called my mother."

God only knew what trouble this was going to start, but the last thing I wanted was to put a damper on her accomplishments. When I assigned her the game plan task, I didn't expect her to start with such extremes. I should have known better.

"I've been thinking about everything." She slammed the paper on the table. "Why should I be such a sap to everyone?"

"You shouldn't." I said. "What did you say to her?"

"I said I was in the hospital and maybe she'd like to visit me."

Oh, how very sad, I thought.

"And I said that I was hurt that she never responds to me."

"What was her reaction?"

"Who knows? She listened, but she didn't say much."

Gracie's sudden changes were too drastic. Her flight into health needed to level off.

"You want to go home tomorrow?" I asked.

"No, I want to go home right now."

"Whoa!" I held up my hands. "Let's slow down just a bit. Tomorrow is a better idea. This has been a crucial two days for you."

"I know you think I'm moving too fast, but I feel great."

"I can see that." I laughed. "But tomorrow will be your day of emancipation."

I was able to catch Phil Corbut in the hall before he started his rounds.

"Glad you're here, Phil. She can go home tomorrow."

A pretty blonde nurse walked by and called out, "Hi there, Doctor Corbut."

"Hi there, yourself," he said, putting his hand to his mouth, Jack

Benny style. "I wish I could remember their names. There are so damn many of them."

"Phil." I snapped my fingers.

"Oh right, sorry...well, fine."

"Thanks for taking care of her."

He shook my hand and winked.

After writing discharge plans in Gracie's chart, I left the hospital. The outside area was well lit but wet fog obscured the parking area. The truck was at the end of the lot. I walked quickly past cars, looking through my purse for the keys. Somebody touched my shoulder.

I yelped involuntarily and turned around to see Eliot Wohlman.

"You startled me," I said. Where were those goddamned keys?

"Sorry. Didn't mean to scare you."

Yeah, right. I was an idiot for not expecting this.

"What do you want?" I said.

Instead of his overcoat, he was wearing an old brown leather jacket. The dimmed light in the parking lot reflected off his eyes. There was no one around. I forced myself to breathe normally.

"You talked her out of seeing me," he said.

"Actually I didn't. She came up with that all by herself. Amazing isn't it?"

"You shouldn't be antagonizing me."

"What are you going to do, Eliot? Disconnect my telephone again? I'm shaking in my boots." Still not finding my keys, I started walking, but he grabbed my arm.

"Take your hand off of me," I said.

He ignored that.

"Take your hand off of me or I'll scream."

He removed his hand from my arm and reached in his pocket.

Out of the corner of my eye, I confirmed again that there was no one around.

Shit.

Neither of us moved. He kept his hand in his pocket.

"You've been after me for years," he said. "First with Jeanne. Now with Gracie."

I slowly put my hand back in my purse. Still no keys. Sweat was dripping down my back. It stung as it got cold. The parking lot was maddeningly empty.

"Do you know why she took the pills?" he said.

I prayed the hand in his pocket was a bluff, trying to make me believe it was a gun.

"Why do you think she did, Eliot? She lived and died for you. You should have seen that."

"No. You should have seen that."

He was right.

"You missed the signs with Jeanne, and you did with Gracie too. What if Gracie tries again, and does it right the next time? The odds are she'll try again. Most suicides are repeaters. It's hard to hear the truth, isn't it? Makes you question everything you're doing."

No one around. Shit. Shit. Shit.

"Jeanne would have turned thirty-two yesterday. Such a lovely girl. She dreamed about having lots of children. And a career in music. Did you know all that?"

"Your cruelty astounds me, Eliot."

"The Dalmane didn't come from her mother. It came from me."

"But the police report..."

"How many times do I have to tell you about my police connections?"

"You knew she would leave you," I said. "So you talked her into taking the pills. You can't bear to have anyone leave you."

"Amateur psychiatry, Sophie."

"You knew how fragile she was. You knew how impressionable, how open to suggestion she could be. What did you say to her?"

He had a smirk on his face.

"How did you do it? Did you tell her she'd never be happy? Did you tell her she'd have nothing but pain and loss for the rest of her life? Did you convince her she was worthless? Useless? What did you say to her?"

He pulled his hand out of his pocket and pointed a gun at me.

"I said that you told me she was a hopeless case."

I was immobilized. Frozen. But then I was mad. I felt a strength building inside me. I felt a power. It came from Jeanne and it came from Elizabeth and yes, it came from Jeremy.

I told the voices of my conscience to get the hell away from me, because I wasn't going to fucking listen to them anymore.

"You're a nothing, Eliot. An inadequate excuse for a man."

"You're not in a good position to say that."

"Put the gun away. There's a security guard thirty feet behind you."

He laughed.

"Put the gun away."

He laughed louder.

"Good evening, Doctor Green. You're working late tonight."

"This man has a gun, Perry."

The guard approached us as Eliot slipped the gun in his pocket.

"What's going on here?" Perry said.

"I want him arrested."

Chapter Eleven

I drove home with my fingers gripping the steering wheel. The icy mist made the driving slippery. The tighter I gripped the wheel, the more the car skidded. Finally, I pulled into our driveway.

Thank you, God. Thank you for getting me home safe.

I called Detective Samms, but I couldn't reach him. I told the operator not to page him. Eliot was in jail, so the whole thing could wait until morning. I had a glass of sherry while I told Dan the details.

"I'd like to just pack us all up and move out of this state," he said. How many of my family members were going to say this to me?

"I know, Dan." We were at the kitchen table. I slid my chair next to his. There was a big bowl of popcorn on the table. "Did you and Robin have a party?" I asked.

"We tried to, but neither of us could get into it."

"Does she talk to you, Dan?"

We both reached for a handful of popcorn at the same time. Instead of taking any, we held hands.

"Sometimes she does."

"You and I haven't taken much time to talk to each other, sweetheart," I said, grabbing some popcorn with my other hand. "Has she told you about wanting to move off-Cape?"

"She's mentioned it. I don't blame her. Most kids want to move out of the state their parents are in."

"I know, but I would just hate it if she left. I should say — I will just hate it when she leaves. I don't ever want her to go."

"What parent doesn't feel that way?" he said. "This part of parenting is universal. It's all pretty predictable." He took some popcorn and fed me. "But it still hurts," he said.

"I bet you think I'm predictable, Daniel," I said, lightheartedly.

"Entirely."

I took some popcorn and fed him.

"And what does the great master of predictability think I'm going to do next?"

He took both of my hands in his. "You're going to fill your mouth with as much popcorn as you can fit in there. Then you're going to pretend to sneeze like you always do."

"Oh really?" And that is precisely what I did. We left the sneezed out popcorn all over the table as we necked. That's when Robin came in, sleepily, and joined the party.

It wasn't until nine o'clock the next morning that I reached Samms.

"We can't hold him," Samms said.

"He had a gun!"

"He had a permit for it."

"Wait a minute. Even with a permit, it's not legal for him to carry it around."

"It is. With what he does for a living, he's entitled to have a special permit."

"But he threatened me with it!" I was hyperventilating already.

"You can come down to the station and press charges. But we can't keep him in jail. He has no prior record. And we have no witnesses to him threatening you."

"But Perry —"

"He didn't hear him actually threaten you. He just took your word for it."

"Is this what really happens? Anybody can point a gun at me and just walk away?"

"Not necessarily. I think you should press charges, but you should know that the case won't come up for several months."

"There's more," I said, and told him about Jeanne. "He made her take the pills. That's murder."

"Not unless you can prove it."

Later, I did go to the police station and file charges. It was incredibly unsatisfying.

I couldn't stand this feeling of being at the mercy of some putz, particularly Eliot.

Dan came home early from work. I was in a sober mood, but

uplifted by seeing my husband. He was always the sunrise in my day. In an attempt to cheer me I assumed, he was carrying two bags of take-out.

"Jesus, Dan. All you think about is food."

He took the bags into the kitchen. He called out, "The boy at the center who doesn't talk finally did."

I ran into the kitchen. "That's unbelievable!"

"I know." He put the bags on the counter and turned around toward me. He folded his arms across his chest, clearly proud of himself. "I never thought anyone would get through to him."

"What did he say?"

"He said he was sorry."

"Sorry? Sorry about what?" I said.

"That's what I asked him. He said he was sorry he didn't talk to me."

"How did you get him to speak in the first place?"

He turned around and began taking things out of the bags and putting them on the table. "By never pressuring him to."

I gave him a big bear hug from behind. "I'm so impressed." He turned and hugged me back, tightly. "So good to feel you around me," I whispered. The moment passed too soon. "Now you have to tell me what wonderful concoctions you bought."

"Well, for Robin, there's pizza. For me, there's pizza, and for you, there's lobster salad."

I pretended to faint while holding the back of my hand to my forehead. "My favorite," I said.

"You say that about any take-out."

"I really mean it this time."

"You always say that, too."

"Dan," I looked over at him. "You're wonderful. All this time, the focus has been on me, and your needs have been tossed aside like yesterday's leftovers," I said.

"Sophie, the only thing I need right now is for us to be safe."

Robin came down the stairs and gave her father a kiss.

"How come I don't get that kind of greeting?" I asked.

"Because you don't bribe me with money like Dad does."

I looked over at Dan who just shook his head. Sometimes my daughter was really a very clever doll. I adored this playful part of her.

"What's for dinner?" She walked past me and to the fridge.

I sang out to her, "I know something you don't know."

"What is it, pizza?"

"Bet yer booties."

She walked by me again, crunching a carrot. "I don't like pizza anymore," she said. "It's too fattening."

I rolled my eyes and looked over at Dan who laughed. Men seem to accept a teenager's rotten comments better than women. They just don't take it personally.

The three of us were puttering in the kitchen when the phone rang. I jumped, but it was my mother.

"How are you?" I said.

"Better."

Dan and Robin had left the kitchen and the pizza box had telekinetically slid toward my hand. A piece of pepperoni was making its way upwards. When I moved the cheese back over the space that once held the pepperoni, you couldn't tell it was missing.

"What's the matter?" I said.

"Don't ask." She was speaking in an odd sounding whisper.

"What's wrong with your voice?"

"Oy, vai iz mir, Sophie."

"Why don't you just tell me, Ma, instead of making me ask you a thousand times?"

"I have a sore throat," she said. "I wanted to ask you about it."

"Ma, we've been over this before. You have to see a doctor when you have physical problems."

She squealed into the phone, "A sore throat, Sophie. I'm not talking hip transplant here."

"Even a sore throat can be serious. I wish you'd listen to me and see a doctor."

"I did."

I closed my eyes. "Why didn't you just say that?"

"You didn't give me a chance." There was silence. My mother was the only person in the world who could pout out loud.

"Well, what did the doctor say?" I asked, carefully relocating another piece of pepperoni to my mouth.

"I didn't pay any attention to what he said because I had to go to one of those drive-through dirty medical centers, where anything can just walk in off the street and plant itself down in the waiting room."

"Where was Doctor Sollows?"

"Where do you think? On vacation when I'm sick."

"Didn't he have someone covering for him?"

"The lady on the phone said that all patients were being referred to the hospital emergency room."

"Then why didn't you go to the hospital?"

"WHAT?" she shrieked. "And sit on some drug addict's blood who just had a car accident? Are you out of your mind, Sophie?"

"All right, Ma." I tried to calm my irritation and slow down. "I understand that you didn't like the doctor at the medical center, but I would like to hear the advice he gave you that you didn't take."

"He said it was just a little irritation and I should gargle with Karo Syrup. Some second rate shnook who can't even finish medical school and has to work at one of these places tells me to gargle with Karo Syrup."

"It sounds like good advice, Ma."

"How would you know? You're a psychiatrist."

I sighed, trying not to make it too loud.

"So how does it feel now?"

"Better. I gargled with honey and lemon like I always told you and Mark to do."

I shut my eyes again. "Well good, Ma. I'm glad to hear you're feeling better."

"I'm not out of the woods yet, Sophie."

She wanted me to worry about her. I felt a great sadness. How much longer would I have a mother, anyway?

"Mom, I..."

The lump in my throat made it impossible for me to talk. Another connection that could be lost forever.

"What were you saying?" she asked.

"I...well, I was saying that I want you to be okay. I need..." I was choked up. "I need you to be okay," I finally got out. I wished I could have told her how much I needed my mother at a time like this, but...I didn't.

We were like two people trapped, each on their own cliff with a steep gorge between us. When one reached out to the other to help her leap across, the other cowered in fear. If we'd both reach out together, we'd get somewhere.

"Ma," I said, "The last time we talked. You wanted to tell me something."

She was quiet for a little bit. "Oh, it was nothing. Just...I don't know what I'd do if you were...sick."

"I'm not sick. The truth of the matter is that one of my patients has been in crisis. It's nothing for you to worry about. Just a lot of extra work for me and that's why I look so tired."

"Why didn't you tell me that to begin with?" she asked.

"I don't know, Ma. I'm sorry."

"You can talk to me sometimes about things that are important, you know."

Didn't I recently say that to Robin?

"I know. I will. I'm really sorry." I covered up another pepperoni hole with a mushroom. There was one slice of green pepper just wide enough to compensate for the next pepperoni that I picked up slowly so as not to spill any of the grease filling the middle.

"So," she said, "what are you making for dinner tonight?"

As of now, each of the twelve slices of pizza had one pepperoni on it. If I went any further, I'd be found out.

"Dan bought pizza for those two and lobster salad for me."

"You should never eat a lobster. You know they eat sewage, don't you?"

"Mo-ther."

"They get if from that pipe coming out of Boston Harbor. Every time a toilet flushes in Boston, it all ends up in a lobster."

It was definitely time for dinner.

"Ma, I'd really like to talk more but I have to go."

"All right, Sophela."

The phone rang just as I hung it up.

"Hello," I said. There was no answer. I hung up and it rang again.

I picked up the receiver and said, "How brave of you, Eliot. Calling and hanging up." There was just a dial tone. I called the special tracing number, but the caller hadn't stayed on long enough.

For some crazy reason, I remained calm. Self protection I guess. I wanted my family around me, so I called everyone in to dine. I shook my head back and forth to clear my brain. Gradually, I pulled myself back into the moment.

Dan zapped the pizza in the microwave and I piled my lobster salad on top of lettuce and tomatoes. There was a bag of no-salt potato chips in the cupboard, which I asked Robin to get.

She looked at the bag with disgust. "Potato chips without salt is just not normal. It's like colorizing *The African Queen*."

Dan looked in the pizza box to see if it was steaming. I was chatting with Robin about movies, but I knew I was just postponing the inevitable.

"Sophie." Here it was. "What happened to the pepperoni?"

"What? Didn't they put any on?"

Robin whined, "I'm not eating any pizza without pepperoni."

"Robin." I was beginning to get a headache. "There will be pepperoni. Every slice has one piece."

At that instant, I realized my error and Dan glared at me victoriously.

"And how did we get that information, dear doctor?"

"No need to be so formal, Dan."

The jig was up. I hung my head in shame. "My mother made me do it."

Minutes later a sharp slam hit the front door. I ran out of the kitchen and rushed to the front door.

"Who's there?" Nothing. Dan and Robin were next to me. I didn't see anyone through the peephole, but you could barely see through it at night anyway. I opened the door slowly.

There was a black plastic garbage bag that was dripping with something dark red. I picked it up; it was heavy. Whatever was inside looked like internal organs, and they seemed to be squirming.

I dropped the bag in horror, but not before Robin saw inside it. She covered her eyes and screamed. "Oh God! Mom!" She was jumping up and down in shock. "Oh God! Oh God! Oh God! Oh God!"

Dan put his arm around her shoulders and led her back in the house while I ran to the kitchen to get the stuff off my hands. Dan sat her down on the couch.

"Okay, sweetie. It's okay now," I said when I returned. I held her to me until I heard her breathing even out a little.

Chapter Twelve

Wednesday, 8:30 PM

Detective Samms arrived within twenty minutes of Dan calling him. He said he had just taken an after dinner walk on the beach and apologized for coming dressed in baggy overalls. I actually thought they were an improvement over his aged suits. He smelled of the ocean. He tracked in sand but I never cared about that which is just as well since everybody on Cape Cod tracked in something from the sea. He took off the herringbone coat and placed it over one of the chairs. The way he gently handled it, you'd think it was a family heirloom. He picked up the disgusting bag and put it outside the door. He said it looked like infested cow entrails. Robin refused to leave the room, of course.

"Who do you think was behind this?" he asked.

"Carl, of course."

He shook his head. "If he was around, we'd know about it. He could be in a different part of the country by now."

"But he could have connections here," I said. "It just fits his profile to do something disgusting like this to scare me and get back at me."

By now, Robin had calmed down. I think she was feeling too overwhelmed. She went to her room. That was just as well.

Samms walked around the living room; his limp grew increasingly pronounced. He took out a silk handkerchief from his pocket and wiped his brow. How he could combine silk with the rest of his ensemble I'll never know.

Desperately needing to do something about my agitation, I asked him if he would take a walk around the neighborhood with me. He said yes. By now it was close to eleven, but I was too wound up to sleep. I got my coat from the closet near the door and told Dan not to worry. We wouldn't be gone long.

The air had its winter bite but there was no wind so it was bearable. In fact, the cold felt good. We both needed to button our coats to our necks. My coat was also a herringbone but made sometime within this century. I was surprised, though, that we shared the same taste in anything, including coat fabrics. My sweat pants looked funny with my coat but I never cared much how I dressed except when I was at the office.

The area was quiet as we walked along the road. There was no sidewalk so we had to walk in the small street which was okay because traffic was sparse. Away from the lights of Hyannis, the stars glistened in their clarity.

The houses in my neighborhood were all variations of the basic Cape Cod style. Most windows had twenty-four panes, twelve over twelve. This added to the old-fashioned look, but were too much of an effort to clean, not that I ever did.

This late, we had the street to ourselves. Everybody's lights were out. We couldn't hear a sound other than our own footsteps in the crisp winter air.

I tried to be friendly. After all, his intentions were good. That much I knew. "Why did you become a detective?"

"You may not agree, but my occupation is a lot like yours."

"I'll have to think about that," I said. "Do you like the work?"

"Yes. I'm a do-gooder. And frankly..." He looked over at me and grinned. "You are, too."

We kept walking, very aware of each other. His pace slowed with the worsening of his limp.

"Since we haven't been snapping at each other for the last two seconds," I said, "I'd like to ask you a personal question."

He shrugged and said, "Go ahead."

"I've been wondering about your knee." I looked straight ahead.

"It's just an old injury. No big deal." An isolated gust of wind made a low howling sound.

We walked further. We passed by a cottage that was over two hundred years old. The village myth was that it was haunted. No one has lived in it for years. People swore that at night they saw a bride in the top window. It gave me a major case of the creeps to walk by it.

"I'm sorry," I said. "I don't mean to hit a raw nerve. I thought it was more than just an old injury. I apologize for prying."

"All right," he said. "This isn't public knowledge, but I know you're used to keeping your mouth shut."

I nodded.

"Before I became a detective, I was patrolling in an area not as fancy as this one." He looked up, recalling the past. "There was one man we used to get frequent calls about. He was a brute, kicked around his kids all the time, but was somehow able to stop protective services from taking over the situation. I guess nobody knew how badly he was hurting them."

A car rambled by slowly. We eyed the young driver suspiciously. He drove away.

"What was he doing to them?"

"Well, there were two. George and David. George was about five and David was thirteen, I think. This was a long time ago. I don't remember for sure."

"That doesn't matter."

"Their dad was pimping for David, I found out later, too much later."

I didn't say anything.

"I guess about the fifth time the wife called us, things had gotten much worse. So I raced over to their house with my siren going. I got into their front door..." His voice cracked.

"I'm sorry." I touched his arm. "You don't have to tell me any more."

"It's all right. I haven't talked about it in a long time. Maybe it's good for me to get it out. Maybe someday I can talk about it without feeling like I'm right there."

We walked.

"In their house...there was junk everywhere, broken glass, trash all around. Sheets and blankets all over the floor. The mother, she was a small woman, was hiding behind the television. She was crying, and holding a bloody towel to her mouth. I had already radioed for help. It looked bad. I brought her out from behind the television and she whimpered and held on to me. When I asked her where her husband was, she got wild in the eyes, and pointed to the bathroom." He stopped walking for a second.

"The bathroom door was closed. I could hear moaning from inside. I put the woman on the couch and went to the door. I gave him a chance to open it, with a warning, but that didn't work. After a couple of seconds, I kicked it in and the father shot me in the knee as the door smashed open. George was in the bathtub crying, and David had his head over the sink. He was bleeding from his mouth. Oddly enough, I didn't feel any pain in my leg. I had my gun out but I didn't shoot then. I told the father to drop his weapon. He put it behind David's head and blew out his brains. If truth be told...I wanted to kill him, and I did."

I realized I was holding my breath, so I forced myself to breathe. "What happened to the other child?"

"George was a mess, emotionally that is. There were two bodies in the bathroom and his mother was in the doorway screaming. I picked him up, out of the bathtub and took him to his mother, but she was too hysterical to take him. So I brought them to the couch in the other room and sat holding George while he cried on my lap. I had my arm around his mother. By this time, other people were arriving and taking care of everything."

"How could you go through such a thing?"

"I don't know the answer to that." We walked the rest of the way in silence. I put my arm through his. By the time we got home, I wasn't so surprised that we had the same taste in coat fabrics.

All through the night, I woke up every hour. Sometime after two o'clock, I got up to go to the bathroom and saw Robin's light on. I put on my slippers and robe and went to her door. I tapped on it. There was no answer so I opened the door and peeked in.

She was wearing her yellow nightgown and appeared to be asleep. She was nestled on her side with her knees up. Her hands were tucked under her chin. I went over to her and bent down to kiss her cheek. It was wet.

"Hi, Mom," she said, her eyes still closed.

I sat on her bed and wiped the tears from her cheek.

"What are you thinking about?"

She looked up at me. "Tonight." She started to cry again. She put her head in my lap. I stroked her hair.

"Pretty horrible, wasn't it?" I said.

"How could anybody do that?"

"I guess some people are very unhappy and they take their

frustration out on other people." She kept crying. I took a tissue from her table and wiped her cheek. I needed one for me too.

"I can't stop thinking about it."

"I know." I stroked her hair.

"Do you know who did it?" she asked.

"I think I do."

"Why can't the police just arrest the person who did it?"

"They will, Robin. When they find him. And they will find him soon."

After a few minutes, I kissed her cheek again and stood to leave.

"Mom?"

I turned back.

"Could you leave the light on?" she asked.

"Sure." I came back to her bed, touched her hair once more and left.

I was furious at whoever was screwing up our lives like this.

Chapter Thirteen

Thursday, 5:30 PM

The day at my office seemed to go on interminably. Oh how I used to love being here.

The harbor looked like a still life painting because there was no wind. I looked out at the water. It was so smooth I could see the reflections of the pilings in the water and a mirror image of the *Pilgrim*.

I knew today would be clear and freezing so I had on my black wool slacks and my white mohair sweater. It only itched when I thought about it.

Across the way, the captain of the *Pilgrim* had untied his boat from the pilings and was beginning to head out of the harbor. He was wearing rain gear — a yellow sou'wester, which I thought was odd because it was a sunny and cloudless day. He looked up at me as his boat passed beneath my window. I saw his eyes from under the yellow rain hood. For a fraction of a second, we connected.

By the time I was through with my day's patients, the rains had begun, and I was ready to ask the captain for a ride.

I had to tell my folks and Mark and Rosie what was going on. I had been procrastinating too long. I sat at my desk called my mother. She started crying.

"Mamala, I'll be fine."

Through her sniffles she said, "You know I couldn't take it if something happened to you."

"I know that, but you've got to try to be strong, Ma. My house is like Fort Knox and Dan's with me all the time. Nothing is going to happen."

Rosie was the only one home when I called over there.

"Sophie, come stay with us. Or at least have Robin come here."

"I may have her come. We'll see."

The only call remaining was a check-in call to Gracie Brill.

"There's something I want to warn you about," she said when I reached her. "Eliot's going to come to your office. He says he's sorry for the other night. He apologized to me too."

As soon as I hung up the phone, there was a knock on the door. Speak of the devil never rang truer. I opened it to find Eliot.

"I need to talk to you," he said. "Just give me one second. I want to apologize for the other night."

"I'm not comfortable having you in here." I inched close to my desk, near the newly installed panic button.

"Don't press that. We can go talk outside if you want."

I remained standing near the desk. He stayed near the door.

"Look, I know I upset you. I wasn't myself. It will never happen again."

"You threatened me with a gun, Eliot."

"We've all done things we wish we could change. Please accept my apology. Please try to understand."

"Get out of here."

"We've both been under a lot of strain," he said.

"There is no excuse for the way you acted or for what you said."

"I agree. I'm just trying to apologize."

"You won't get away with it. You might as well kiss your career good-bye."

"Please!" He crumpled to the floor and put his hands over his eyes.

"What are you doing?"

"I'm begging you," he said. "Try to understand."

"I do understand." He'd be shocked to hear what I had done. Pressing charges for aiming a gun at me was only the beginning. I intended to see him pay for aiding and abetting the destruction of Jeanne's life. "I've already called the state licensing board," I said, so proud of myself for having taken that step. "They've begun an investigation. They're interviewing staff at your clinic, and they're confiscating your patients' files. They asked me to testify against you at an inquiry, and I've set the date."

He stood up and brushed off his pants. He was livid.

"As soon as I testify, they'll pull your license."

"It takes years to have a license revoked," he said.

"That's right, and that's fine with me, because while the whole process is going on, you're not going to be allowed to practice in Massachusetts."

"I could leave the state."

"Good riddance."

"Why are you destroying me?"

"I wish I could accept the honor, but it's all yours."

In a fury, he spun around and left the office.

On my ride home with Dan, I described the scenario.

"I want to be in the waiting room when there's anyone around that you have the slightest concern about. I don't want to be at the center or right outside in the parking lot while you're in danger. Jesus, Sophie."

"I didn't know he'd be there. He could come any time."

We sat in silence, holding hands between the curves, on the dark ride home. Driving down Route 6A, we passed the old captain's houses. I looked up to see the widows' walks on top of each one — where the waiting wives could see the ocean and hopefully the return of their husbands' ships. I thought how insignificant my problems really were, when it came to my tiny moment in history. But I bet the captains' wives felt the same dread that I did of what could lie ahead.

Chapter Fourteen

Saturday, 9 AM

Saturday morning brought a snow storm — a rare occurrence on the Cape. The surrounding ocean's warm air usually kept the snows at bay. Bundling up in front of the woodstove for the whole day would have been great, but we had a date with Mark and Rosie. I didn't think I could pull it off. Not today.

"Could you call them and get us out of it?" I said to Dan. "Please?"

"What should I say?"

I thought for a minute. My family was already agonizing over me and this would make it worse.

"No," I said at last. "Let's go, but let's just keep it short."

Dan drove the Blazer expertly through the snow to Mark's house. It was a twenty minute drive. He chose this time to check in with Robin, who was in the back seat.

"What do you like doing the most?" he said.

"I don't know."

I watched the old Cape homes as we passed by — so beautiful in the snow. Even the short and stubby pitch pines topped in white looked like a New England dream scene.

"If you answer something other than, 'I don't know'," Dan said, "I'll give you five bucks."

Bribing an adolescent for a response was not my idea of effective parenting and I gave him a look that told him so.

Robin laughed and said, "You mean that, Dad?"

He said, "Yes," and asked me for five dollars.

"Oh no you don't," I said. "I'm not participating in this."

"Too late. You're already participating in it, only you're the only one being negative," he said.

We passed by an ancient cemetery that we've walked through in different seasons. It held the remains of sea captains and their families. I've seen many of the tombstones where the husbands predeceased their wives and I thought about the widows' last agonizing wait for their men to come home from the sea. Most of the grave markers were simple gray slates. Time had affected their stature and they were all leaning in different directions. Today, each one had a peak of snow.

Robin was giggling in the back seat. If anyone had looked at us in the car, they would have seen a father and daughter laughing and a wife looking grimly out the window. What a picture.

"If you give her money now," I said, "she'll always expect something."

"No she won't, will you, Robin?"

"No way, Dad."

"For Christ's sake," I said, and found a five dollar bill in my purse.

"All right, Robin." I waved the bill in front of her. "What's your eloquent response?"

"What was the question again?" she asked, getting quite a big kick out of herself.

I wasn't in the mood for any of this. "Robin, please, your father wanted to know, um...oh damn, what was the stupid question, Dan?"

"Tell me two things you like to do and that five spot is yours," he said.

"No fair, Dad. You said one thing. For two, I'm getting ten dollars."

"So you do remember the question," he said, "you cheating sack of poop."

"Dan!" I yelled.

"Okay Dad," she said. "I'll answer two, but Mom has to give me the money first."

"Robin, just answer the damn question."

"I like that," Dan said. "Do you think Doctor Spock would prefer your way or mine?"

Finally Robin managed to answer. "I like to cross country ski and I like to speak French."

By this time, we were pulling into my brother's driveway.

"Well put." Dan snatched the five dollars out of my hand. In an elaborate magnanimous gesture, he presented the money to her.

"Thanks, Dad."

I closed my purse and gave them a look.

I was trying to talk myself into believing that it would be a good idea to be here today. Maybe it would relax me.

Mark and Rosie lived in a larger house than we did, but it was built in the same gray-shingled style. Their backyard was twice the size of ours. Everything my brother had was either newer or larger than what we had. But sibling rivalry was such an ugly thing. Such a lowly pursuit was far beneath me.

"Exactly how much land do you have, Mark?" I asked.

Dan elbowed me. We were taking our coats off in the foyer. "I was just curious," I snarled.

"Sophie," Mark whispered. "Are they closer to finding Carl?"

"Not now, Mark. Let's not discuss it. Nothing's new anyway. Just tell me how much land you have."

"Oh, about two acres. Why?"

"No reason." I hung our coats in the closet. "Dan," I whispered, "exactly how much land do we have?"

"Sophie, please. You're acting like a five-year-old."

Mark and Rosie were bustling about in the kitchen and couldn't hear us.

I stomped my foot. "Just tell me. How much land do we have?"

"We have almost one acre. I've told you a million times."

He walked toward the kitchen, but I yanked him back by his elbow.

"But how much if we include that marshy area in the back?"

"We don't own that."

"Yeah, but no one can build on it anyway, so we might as well consider it a part of our property, right?"

"Wrong." He pulled his arm away. "And I'm not going to discuss this any further." We went into the kitchen where Mark had draped a sheet over something the size of a dishwasher. Their kitchen was spotless. All the appliances were shiny black. Only useful things hung on the wall — a clock and a calendar. A rack to hold knives. The windows, Anderson of course, had bright white perfectly clean horizontal slatted blinds.

Rosie was wearing a hand-knitted white sweater and a long wool peach-colored skirt. The black glasses really stood out. She put her arm around my shoulder. "How are you doing?" she said.

"I'm okay. It's good to be here and get a break from it all."

Mark wore a tie with his brown wool cardigan. Dan, Robin, and I all had on dungarees and old sweaters.

"I didn't know we were dressing up," I said.

"Don't worry about it," Rosie said. "Not everybody shares Mark's excitement about trash compactors." She lifted the sheet, but Mark took it out of her hand and put the sheet back, carefully smoothing out the wrinkles.

She turned my way and we gave each other a knowing glance. Mine said that we loved him in spite of the fact that he was a ding-dong. I thought her look said the same, and I was hoping that she wasn't embarrassed about his weirdness in front of me. She never opened up to me.

Mark presided over us like a rabbi at an unveiling. We gathered around solemnly. He ceremoniously flung off the sheet.

Nobody moved.

What do you think?" he asked.

"Great," Dan said.

He turned to me. I was afraid of this. "What do you think of it, sis?"

I really didn't want to hurt his feelings, so I said, "It's really nice. Why don't we take a look inside?"

"I thought you'd never ask!" He slid the trash compartment out from the unit.

The five of us stood around it and peered in. There was a paper towel on the bottom with what looked like mustard on it.

We kept peering in. Again, no one moved.

My lower back was starting to hurt.

"Well," Mark said, "I know you didn't come here just to stand around a trash compactor." He clapped his hands twice and we all straightened up. Thank God, there was going to be an end to this. I began to imagine all the wonderful exotic treats Rosie had prepared for us when I saw my brother go out the back door and bring in a heavy looking garbage can full of trash.

Robin, trying to suppress laughter, did a quick turn and sped out of the room in the direction of the bathroom.

"We'll wait for you to get through in the bathroom, dear," Rosie called after her.

"No, that's okay," she managed to get out.

"Oh no, Robin," I called. "We wouldn't think of letting you miss all the fun."

In less than a minute, I heard the toilet flush and Robin came back into the kitchen giving me an I'm going to kill you, Mom, look.

"Ready?" Mark waited until he got a nod from all of us.

He hoisted the trashcan with Dan's help. Then he slid the trash holder back into the unit and latched it shut. Before he pressed the ON button, he stood motionless with his finger just a hair away from the button.

Again, we waited. Robin snorted. Mark looked over at her. "Sorry, Uncle Mark, I have something in my throat." She looked over at me. Her face was bright red.

"Just do it," Rosie said.

He pressed the button and we listened to the machine make noise for about twenty seconds.

I looked out the kitchen window. The snow was still coming down outside. I dearly needed to be home. It didn't feel right to be here, at my brother's house, while my life was falling apart. But I wanted to be cheerful for my family.

"An orgasmic experience," I said, and Robin laughed out loud.

Rosie went to the fridge and began bringing out platters of goodies. There were two kinds of bite-size round quiches. One was spinach, the other mushroom and tomato. She had a tray of Ritz crackers topped with cream cheese with a little dab of mint jelly on each one.

We all sat around their black Formica kitchen table admiring her work.

I took a bite of the hot spinach quiche. It was heavenly, all gooey with spinach and onions swimming in thick mozzarella cheese. "Oh Rosie," I said, "so good, so good."

"What's this, Aunt Rosie?" Robin pointed to the Ritz crackers.

"I'm not telling, Robin," she teased. "Just try it."

"It's green," she said.

I kicked her under the table. "What's wrong with green?" I asked.

She looked at me and said, "Think about it, Mom."

I didn't want to do that.

There was a knock on the door and I jumped. A common reaction these days.

Mark said, "I told the folks to stop by anytime this afternoon."

Rosie went to the door, but it wasn't my folks. I could see her bending over to pick up a box on her front step.

Without rushing and making my fear obvious to anyone else, I went to the door and took Rosie's arm. "Don't open that," I whispered, and grabbed the small box. It was flat and wrapped in dark red paper.

"I wasn't going to," she said. "It says it's for you." And she handed me a little white card that said "For Doctor Green" in block letters.

"Bring everybody in," Mark called out from the kitchen.

"It wasn't the folks, Mark," I called back. "It was just…just um, just a religious couple."

"I don't think you should open this," Rosie said. I knew intellectually she was right, but my simmering emotions took over. Sick and tired of being the victim of someone else's crap, I tore it open. Inside was a photograph of Robin, recently taken. She was crossing the street in front of the house to get the newspaper, wearing a ski parka over her nightgown.

"What is it?" Rosie asked urgently.

I stuck the box and the photo in my pocket before she could see. "It's not good," I said. "I'll take care of it."

"But what is it?"

I touched her arm. "Rosie, I can't tell you what it is. You know that a lot of bad things have been happening. This person's just trying to scare me and I don't want to show it to you. That wouldn't help anything if I did. I'm going to take it to the detective. Just do me a big favor and don't say anything to anyone right now. Please?" I pleaded.

She thought for a moment, then nodded her head reluctantly. I really appreciated the kinship. We walked back together to the kitchen.

There was another knock on the door. This time it was the folks.

Rosie went to fetch them. They came in arguing.

"How could you drive like a crazy person through this blizzard, Milton? You were deliberately trying to scare me to death."

"It's only two inches of snow, for crying out loud, and my driving was fine."

"Then you should have your eyesight checked." She took off three scarves, all navy blue, and draped them over a metal stool. Then, she took off her blue wool coat and blue wool sweater. After that came her rubbers. She picked up the whole pile and deposited it in the living room. When she returned, her mood had improved. The seven of us exchanged kisses.

"Hi Ma," I said, as I hugged her. I forced myself to put the photo out of my mind. "How's the throat?"

"Fine. It was nothing. Just a sore throat." She looked closely at me. "Sophie, you've got more gray hairs."

Only a mother can say hello like that.

She looked over the food on the table, gave a few sniffs and sat down. "Nobody is good enough to deserve a cook like you, Rosie, not even my own son."

Rosie beamed.

"What's wrong with these?" She pointed to the cracker-cream cheese-mint jelly platter, because it looked like it hadn't been touched.

"Don't ask," Robin said.

My dad changed the subject. "So how's it going at the center?" he asked Dan. "You still like working with those teenagers?"

"I do," he said. "It's not always going so great on a day to day basis, but in the long run, I think it's good for the kids to have some place to go after school. But I'd say only about half of them like to be there."

"You shouldn't be working with juvenile delinquents," my mother said. "They'll just steal your money and buy dirty pictures with it."

The party ended around three o'clock. Rosie gave us all leftovers. My mother asked me to walk with her to their car.

"I have something for you," she said.

It was still snowing and I held her arm to keep her from falling on the slippery driveway. She opened the door and picked up a package from her seat.

"This was my mother's and now I want you to have it."

I opened the small cardboard box. Inside was a single brass candlestick, about four inches tall, shaped like a princess — her crown being the candle holder. Her hem was lined with tiny china roses. It was exquisite.

"Why are you giving this to me now?"

"I want to help, but I don't know how. I can at least give you something."

Sprinkles of snow came down around my mother's gift, giving it a look of one of those glass balls with ballerinas or snow scenes in them that you shake to make the snow particles float all around.

"Thank you, Ma. I love it." We hugged each other and I thought she was trying not to cry, the same way I was trying. "I love you, mamala."

"I love you too."

We slowly made our way home through the snow. I called Samms about the picture of Robin. He said he'd pick it up, which he did, about ten minutes after we got in the door. He didn't appear the least surprised about it. I spent the remainder of the weekend in my nightgown, reading psychiatric journals and *People Magazine*.

Chapter Fifteen

Monday, 10 AM

By the time Monday arrived, my twenty-four hour migraine had begun to go away. I sat in my office and stared out the window. The snow was almost gone from Saturday's storm. Sunlight glistened on the ice on the pilings. It looked like layers of whipped cream. I was wearing my only light-colored sweater, pink and yellow, with my matching yellow skirt. I usually received compliments when I wore something other than black on black.

Gracie Brill arrived for her appointment looking super, wearing a blue velour exercise outfit.

"Doctor Green." She sat down. "There's something I have to tell you. If I don't say it now, I never will."

"Go ahead."

"I...I was arrested before. I didn't tell you the truth when you asked me."

"I know all about it."

"What?"

"When that detective looked up everybody's record, he found out about what happened and told me about it."

"You mean you've known all along?"

"For a while."

"Aren't you angry at me?"

"No, Gracie. You're under no obligation to tell me anything you don't want to."

"Did he say I was told to see a therapist?"

"Yes."

"I feel like I owe you an explanation about what happened."

"You don't."

"But I want to tell you about it. Brad, um, Brad Philbrick, that doctor, he wasn't molesting his patients. He loved his patients like family. Everybody took it all wrong." She was momentarily quiet. "And around that time, well, that's the time I started to tell you about in the hospital. I tried to…"

"You tried to commit suicide." We just needed to say the word.

"Yes, I…I tried to…I took pills, but I threw up. Brad took care of me." She looked embarrassed. "I won't do it again." She continued, "I'm not sorry I went after the patient who started the whole thing."

"I was surprised you decked her."

"Well, I didn't get a chance to really hurt her, but I wanted to. She ruined his life. He'll never practice again. He's somewhere in Florida now. I don't know what he's doing."

"Gracie, are you that sure he wasn't guilty? I remember at least five women coming forward."

"He was framed. The lawyers contacted his patients and asked them to testify. They put words in their mouths."

"Who told you that?"

"He did. I just know he would never have done the things they said he did."

She looked at the sea, lost in thought.

"I feel so much better that I ended it with Eliot," she said. "My life is finally going to turn around." It was good to see her so sure of herself.

We watched a sea gull soar above the ice-making plant on the other side of the harbor. He dropped a clam onto the metal roof and swooped down to eat the now available insides.

"I wrote a letter to my mother." She reached into her purse and took it out.

"Would you like me to read it?"

"Yes, if you would. I'd like that very much."

On a piece of yellow stationery with tiny daisies around the border, she had written:

> Dear Mom,
> I am writing this letter because I want to say some things that I haven't been able to say before. This is hard for me to do. I've always been afraid to express my feelings, especially to you. But now I'm not afraid anymore.

It hurts me that you don't want anything to do with me. Every time I send you a card or a present, you don't answer me and when I call, you're always too busy to talk to me.

I have recently realized that I definitely don't deserve to be unloved this way. I never did anything to deserve your neglect.

So this is good-bye. Believe me, it's the hardest thing I've ever said but I do mean it.

Good-bye,

Gracie

P.S.

If you want to talk any of this over, I'm free weekday nights after six o'clock.

"That's quite a powerful letter," I said. "You are a brave woman."

"I couldn't have done it without you."

"I'm not taking the credit. You wrote the letter. You're making some fundamental changes." Oh how wonderful it was when a patient began to soar. Psychotherapy was sometimes as good for the therapist as it was for the patient.

All too soon for both of us, her hour came to a close. The clock chimed six times. She slowly got up and went to the door.

"I suppose you know what I'm going to say," she said.

"Not really." But I did.

"Thank you."

"I'm glad to help, Gracie."

"I thank you so much — for everything."

I smiled at her as she strode out the door.

It wasn't until five thirty that I finished work. My last person was my compulsive eating patient. By that time, I wanted to ball up a whole loaf of white bread and fit it into my mouth, which I actually did once, in college, on a bet.

Dan came into the waiting room with Robin. "What a surprise," I said.

"Dad asked me to come along."

They were bundled in parkas, scarves, hats and gloves.

"I thought it might be good for us if we took a walk around the point and then went to Jake's for subs," Dan said. He was carrying pants and boots and a jacket for me.

"Sounds good," I said. "How about we skip the walk and just eat?"

"Come on, Sophie, you need the exercise."

I quickly changed into the pants and zipped up the parka. "Why do you say that?"

"Don't start. Exercise is a great stress reliever. That's all I meant."

I gave him a dirty look and grabbed the gloves.

We trundled out to the parking lot. I looked around, but the place was deserted. We came to a path that took us to the water's edge. The wind chill made it feel like it was only fifteen degrees out. We walked away from the office building for five minutes and came to a point of land. Straight ahead, across the bay, stretched Sandy Neck, a six-mile long spit of sand dunes and pitch pines. The water was choppy and black. We walked to the right a quarter of a mile with the ocean on our left. No one spoke. It was too cold and windy. When we made a complete circle around and up the road to my building, it was fully dark.

We were all shivering when we climbed into the Blazer.

"There, wasn't that refreshing?" Dan started the engine and turned on the heat.

Robin was quiet in the back.

"You okay, sweets?" I asked.

"Just freezing to death."

I didn't believe her. Something was wrong.

We drove to Jake's in Hyannis, which was about ten minutes from our house. It's a local hangout, known for their pizza. On this cold, wintry night, the place was almost empty. There were half a dozen kids playing video games and three couples sitting together sharing large pizzas and a pitcher of beer.

We took off our coats and sat at a table that was covered with a red checkered cloth. I saw two workmen sitting at the bar, drinking shots of whiskey with beer chasers.

No one noticed us come in.

"We have to start with stuffed quahogs," I said.

"I'll order them," Dan said. "You too, Robin?"

"Yeah, thanks."

A few minutes later, a young skinny waitress brought us three steaming quahogs with Tabasco sauce on the side. The chopped clams were mixed to perfection with onions and bread crumbs and linguica. We ate and looked at the menu. Then, we all ordered subs.

"Are you serving pizza by the slice?" I asked our waitress while she took our order.

"We have plain and pepperoni by the slice. A dollar fifty each," she said.

"I'll have plain," Robin said.

"And I'll have pepperoni," I chimed in. "And Dan, you have to have one or you'll make us feel like gluttons."

"I'll have a plain slice," he said.

"And we'd like one large order of fries and one large order of onion rings and three Diet Cokes," I said.

"I'm off Diet Coke, Mom. It's made of chemicals."

"Well, what would you like?"

"Water," she said.

I had the feeling she had a hidden agenda tonight.

The waitress brought our dinner. My steak sub was loaded with sautéed onions, peppers, mushrooms and slathered with mayo. The old "food will take you away from all this" drug was rearing its lovely head.

"Robin," I said, an onion dangling from my mouth. "Is everything okay?"

She breathed a Green family sigh. Daintily, she took a tiny French fry and ate it plain. "Well," she said. Another fry. "There's something I want to tell you, but I don't want you to make a big deal out of it the way you do everything, Mom."

"What?"

"I've been sort of seeing a counselor." She couldn't look at either of us.

The onion dropped to the plate. "You're WHAT?"

"Mom." She looked down. "You heard me. I've told you I haven't been happy."

"You're seeing a counselor?" I screeched. The workmen at the bar turned around.

"It's no big deal. She's the school psychologist and there's nothing wrong with me going. I like talking to her about how I feel. A lot of kids at school talk to her."

"But...but..." I couldn't get the words out. "You're telling some stranger all about your family's private business?"

"Pull yourself together," Dan said to me, "and try to remember what you do for a living."

"Mom, you're making me feel ashamed for seeing her."

Oh God. She was right.

"I'm sorry, honey," I said, and started on the onion rings.

Dan patted her on the shoulder. "I am proud of you. It takes guts to go to a counselor, and you made this decision on your own. You recognized there was a problem and you're taking steps to solve it. Good for you, Robin." He turned toward me. "Don't you have something to say to her, Sophie?"

"What do you talk about?" I said.

"Sophie!" Dan said. "Therapy is private and between the counselor and the patient."

"You're right," I said. "Sorry." We continued munching our subs.

Dan turned to me, "Why don't we change the subject and just be happy that Robin is taking care of herself?"

"I am happy, really. Robin, I'm happy."

"Good, Mom."

I started on the pepperoni pizza. "Who do you talk about more, me or your father?"

"Sophie," Dan warned.

"Mom, did it ever occur to you that I may have other things to talk about in my life besides you and Dad?"

"I know, Robin. Of course you do. I feel terrible I reacted badly. I am truly very, very proud of you."

"Good. Now let's talk about something else," Dan said.

"I suppose you told her about the time I was too tired to make you pancakes and you cut your finger in the blender when you tried to make them yourself?"

In unison, Robin said, "Mo-ther!" and Dan said, "Soph-ie!"

"Sorry." I hit my forehead with my palm. "That's the last comment I'll make."

We managed to declare a truce, or more specifically, we made a deal that I was never to discuss the counseling again, because I obviously couldn't handle it.

The shrill ring of the telephone woke me out of an already fitful sleep at seven-thirty in the morning. I knew it meant trouble.

"Hello?" I could barely get the word out.

"Doctor Green?"

"Yes."

"This is a tracer call from your answering service. A Doctor Phillip Corbut wants you to meet him at the hospital as soon as you can. He said one of your patients has been admitted this morning.

"Did he say who?"

"No, he didn't."

I hung up and called the hospital, but Phil didn't answer his page.

I woke Dan. "I have to get to the hospital before work."

"I'll drive you," he said sleepily. "You're not driving by yourself again."

"Good."

We showered together, something we hadn't done in weeks, then got dressed. I woke Robin and reminded her to put the burglar alarm back on when she left for school. Having that installed made me more comfortable, but not much. I felt better when she was safely in school, surrounded by hundreds of people.

I was at the hospital at eight-thirty.

Phil was at the nurses' station on the third floor.

"It's Gracie Brill," he said.

"What?"

"A jogger found her in her car on a dirt road in the Barnstable conservation land. It was another suicide attempt. Her car was running and there was a hose connected from the muffler going into the front window. She's still in a coma, and I've got her on one hundred percent oxygen. I'm not sure she'll make it."

"Phil," I said, "do you really think she'll die?"

"I don't know."

"It can't be suicide. I mean, I just saw her yesterday."

"But you had just seen her the same day on the first attempt."

"Yes — but I just know there's no way she would do this."

"What can I say?" He put his hands in the air. "I'm just telling you what I know. There's no evidence that it happened any other way than it looks."

"I'll go see her," I said, and left.

Something was drastically wrong here. There wasn't one hint that she'd try again. If anything, it was just the opposite. Somebody else was involved somehow. She wouldn't do this again — not now.

You should have seen this coming.

There was nothing to see coming, I shouted in my head to my vile conscience.

Please, God, don't let her die. I know you hear this all the time, but please be there for this girl.

Gracie was lying in bed, unconscious. There was an IV hooked up to her arm, and she had on an oxygen mask. She didn't respond for the ten minutes I examined her. I squeezed her fingers, rubbed her chest. Nothing. I decided to go with my intuition and get Detective Samms involved. It was a matter of life and death.

After writing a few quick notes in her chart, I went back to the nurses' station. There was no need to talk to Phil right now. I handed the chart across the desk.

Dan was in front of the hospital waiting for me. "The day is already a disaster," I said and got into the Blazer. "I'm going to call Samms and see if he can meet me at the office at two. Want to come?"

"Definitely," he said.

On the way to the harbor, I filled him in on the latest. He didn't want to leave me alone at the office and insisted on staying in the waiting room all morning.

"You have to go to work, Dan. You can't stay by my side forever."

"What would you want to do if I was in danger?"

"Stay by your side forever."

"I'll run over there while you're in session. But then I'll be back." I didn't fight him.

I had to pull myself together for a ten o'clock session with Charlie. He had asked to have his two o'clock appointment changed to ten, implying that it was urgent. It's been so unlike him to alter the time structure of his appointments.

By the time he arrived, I had decided to reschedule my afternoon people.

Charlie came in, disheveled. He wasn't wearing his standard three-piece suit. He was wearing what looked like green army pants with the same kind of shirt.

"I am considering not coming to therapy anymore, Doctor Green."

Shit. What the hell was going on? "That's fine, Charlie. Could you please tell me what has made you consider this?"

He cleared his throat seven times. "I don't need to work on my problem of leaving my mother, now that she's gone."

"Well, that's true."

"So there's really no point in my being here."

But then, abruptly his formal mood changed, and he looked like he was trying very hard to bring himself to say something.

"You can say whatever you want Charlie."

He cleared his throat again. He kept trying to speak, but then would stop himself. After several anguishing attempts, he finally blurted out, "Do you have feelings for me at all, Doctor Green?"

"Well, of course I do. I care about what happens to you."

"No, that's not what I mean." He took off his glasses and blew something like a hair off of them. Then he smiled a very sweet, but pathetic smile. "I like you…very much," he said.

"I like you too." I was becoming scared. Of course he could hurt me. Who was I kidding being so certain that he couldn't all this time?

"I don't think you understand what I'm trying to say," he said.

I knew what he was trying to say, and I had to deal with it.

"Yes, Charlie. I think I know what you're saying. The feelings you have for me are very normal and nothing to be ashamed of. Here we sit together each week and talk about matters of your heart. It's only natural that you would develop strong feelings toward me."

"So wouldn't it be natural for you to have the same feelings toward me?"

Oh boy. How do I answer him truthfully and not crush him at the same time? Or worse — make him angry.

"Well, not really. You see, I think of my therapy relationships as purely professional." I could see that stung him. "I feel that way with all my patients. Even if someone was charming and a very, very fine person like you are, I keep a distance. I wouldn't be able to help people if I wanted a different kind of involvement with them. I'd have my own interests in mind and I wouldn't be able to be objective."

There were lots of gray areas here, I knew. With Gracie, for instance. I'm acutely aware of my maternal feelings toward her.

"I wouldn't respect myself as a psychiatrist if I let romantic feelings enter into the sessions."

"I, well, I guess if I stopped coming here, I wouldn't see you anymore."

"No, Charlie. You wouldn't."

He did not want to deal with his OCD and how it ruled his life. He wasn't going to touch that subject, and therefore neither would I. If I did at this juncture, it would never work. He'd resist treatment. First, because he's never wanted to put a stop to his symptoms to begin with and second, because if he decided to continue therapy to get a handle on them, he'd no longer need to see me when he did. That treatment goal would be a set up for failure. Therapy would only work if he ever made the decision that he wanted to curb his symptoms because they were intolerable. But now, with the two most important women in his life gone — me and his mother — curbing his life structuring rituals would be the last thing he'd want to do. And the last thing I'd want him to do, I had to admit.

At the close of our hour, he stood up to leave. I stood up too, to shake his hand. I should have known better. He never shook anyone's hand because of germs. It was a terribly awkward moment as I held my hand out. He looked at it, and in slow motion, finally took my hand for a shake, but within a tiny second, withdrew his hand. He smiled that sweet smile again and thanked me. "I know I'm not supposed to say this, Doctor Green, but I can't imagine life without seeing you again." He continued to stand there and stare at me. "I can't help but wonder something."

"Go ahead, Charlie. You can tell me." We were both standing by the door.

"If you hadn't pushed me to tell my mother I was thinking of leaving, she would still be alive today."

I didn't get a chance to respond. He quickly wiped the door handle with his tissue and left.

Oh Jesus, no. Charlie blamed me for his mother's death. What the hell was he planning on doing about that? And now I wouldn't have the chance to help him see otherwise. What a mess. And what a bad way to end therapy. I sat at my desk and thought about it. I truly didn't want to see him again — ever. But that wasn't right. I decided I would give it a few days, and call him to say that I think it would be in his best interests, therapeutically, if we had one more session. He will probably imagine that I'm responding to his romantic quest. But I just couldn't let it end this way. God knows what I was setting myself up for by seeing him again. But I couldn't live with myself if I didn't do the right thing. I prayed my fears about him were all in my mind. It was natural for me to imagine that everybody was after me. "It's natural, right?" I said silently to my brain. But I didn't hear any answer.

I did feel a little better having decided this and wrote down my treatment plan. Then, with my usual trepidation of late, I opened the door to the waiting room. I was thrilled that Dan was there. I plopped myself on his lap, squishing his *Mother Earth News*.

"Did you reach Samms?" he asked.

"Yeah, he'll be here at two. I'm going to reschedule my remaining people so if you want to keep reading your magazine and bone up on joining a commune, I'll go try to reach them."

I was able to reach everybody. Otherwise, I would have had to put a note on my door.

I checked in with the answering service and found one message. Doctor Henry Broussard wanted me to call him at the hospital.

Now what?

I was getting a headache again. Henry was in administration at Hyannis Hospital. I was put right through to him.

"Sophie?"

"What's up?"

"We need to talk. When is the soonest you could get here?"

I looked at my watch, eleven-fifteen. I could be there by eleven-thirty, which should give me enough time before my meeting with Samms.

"Henry, please. Can't you tell me what this is about? I'm already having a bad day."

"I don't want to do this over the phone."

"All right," I said, "I can be there in fifteen minutes if I leave right now."

"Good."

I hung up the phone and called to Dan, "You won't believe this."

He came in the office and sat down with his crumpled magazine.

"Henry Broussard wants to meet with me now. He's the head administrator at the hospital."

"Now?" he asked.

"He wouldn't tell me what it was about and I'll go nuts if I don't know right away."

Fifteen minutes later we pulled up to the hospital's main entrance. "I'll be in this area," he said.

"Sweetheart," I took his hand. "Your kids are going to think it's really weird that you're never there lately."

"No they won't."

"How have you explained your absence?"

"I told them the truth."

"You what? What did you say?"

"I said that my wife has had threats made toward her by one of her patients and that I was going to spend as much time with her as I could."

"What an ingenious idea," I said. "Telling adolescents the truth. You could make a fortune writing a book on that."

He squeezed my hand then let it go. "Don't worry about the center. Now go and see what's going on with Henry."

I looked at him in amazement. "What would I do without you? Saying 'thank you' sounds so stupid." We kissed. As I was about to close the door, he held my arm. I looked at my husband, his face full of love. "I know," I said. "I feel the same way too." In silence, we communicated a lifetime of feelings.

Then he drove away.

Henry's office was on the first floor and he was sitting behind his desk with the door open, waiting for me. He was a tall hefty man with white hair that looked whiter because of his fluffy black eyebrows.

"Come in, Sophie." He stood up and gave me a handshake. "You look tired."

"I know. Everything always happens at once, doesn't it?" That was just a rhetorical question but he picked up on it.

"What is everything?" he asked.

"Oh, several of my patients are having a tough time. Things never seem to occur in neat manageable intervals."

"I understand one of your patients has been admitted twice," he said.

"Yes." I was feeling my paranoia taking its grip, so I got to the point. "What's the problem? Why did you call me?"

"Sophie." He reached in his left pocket for an imaginary pack of cigarettes. I've seen many male ex-smokers do that. "There's something I wanted to talk with you about."

"I know." I tried to stay calm. "Would you please tell me what it is?"

"I'm getting some pressure." He stopped talking.

"What sort of pressure?"

Again, he reached for the pocket. I wished I had a cigarette to give him so he'd get on with it.

"This patient of yours, Gracie Brill, had just recently tried to kill herself."

"You read her chart?" I asked.

"I did," he went on, "and she's in here today on a second attempt. Not only that, it doesn't add credibility to your treatment that she has a history of at least one other attempt." He waited for my reaction.

"And?"

"Some people are questioning your judgment. It looks like you released a patient prematurely, and sent her back to her home where she lives alone. Perhaps you should have sent her to an inpatient psych facility or perhaps you should have kept her here. Either way, if the girl dies, it looks pretty bad for the hospital that one of our staff psychiatrists misjudged and released an actively suicidal person. And..." again with the pocket, "if she recovers, it still looks bad."

"This isn't from Phil Corbut, is it?" I said.

"No."

"Who started all this?" I asked.

"I'm sorry, I can't tell you that."

"Christ, Henry," I said.

"Look, we're old pals," he said. "We've known each other over ten years. I'm telling you this to do you a favor. I don't know whether you were right or wrong, but I want you to be aware of what's going on. If she dies, we could all be sitting in the middle of a malpractice suit."

"You're not talking about suspending my privileges here, are you?" I asked.

"Not yet."

It didn't take me long to realize that Eliot was setting me up. He could easily waltz in here and read a medical chart. "You know I'm having Eliot Wohlman investigated, Henry. Is that who's behind this?"

"I can't tell you that. I wish I could."

"Who are you thinking of that could sue?" I asked.

"The girl has a mother somewhere, I understand. It wouldn't be an open and shut negligence case, but I have to be frank. It would be pretty close to one."

We were silent.

"I'm not going to defend myself to you," I said.

"I'm not asking you to."

"I will say I don't believe I acted wrongly."

"But the girl was obviously not stabilized. You have to admit that," he said.

"It would appear that way...if in fact this was a suicide attempt."

"What are you getting at?"

"I think she was forced."

"You mean someone tried to kill her?" he asked.

"That's exactly what I mean."

"Oh, brother," he said, and reached for his pocket. "Why would someone want her dead?"

"I can't discuss her relationships with you, Henry."

Henry's face was reddening. Looked like he wasn't keeping up with his blood pressure medicine.

I stood up. "I have to go."

He stood also. "What's going to happen now?"

"I'll take care that. Just count your blessings you're not in my shoes."

As I turned to leave, he said, "For what it's worth, you've always been a well-liked and highly respected psychiatrist around here."

"Thanks, Henry. That's worth a lot." I turned and left.

Chapter Sixteen

Tuesday, 1 PM

I found Dan in the Blazer, then cried the whole way to the office. He had bought me a tuna sandwich and a milk from the cafeteria. I couldn't eat.

At two o'clock, Samms arrived. With Dan's input, I filled him in on the latest developments.

"I have reasonable cause to believe that foul play was involved with Gracie," I said.

"Frankly, I think we've got more to worry about with Elizabeth's husband. Your first case, Gracie, is all supposition. Your second is fact. Carl has already come after you twice."

"I'm not saying that I'm not scared about Carl. Believe me, I'm terrified," I said. "But I think we've got equal problems with whoever did this to Gracie."

"You're presuming."

"Of course I'm presuming, for God's sake," I said. "That's what I do for a living."

"All right." He sat back in the wingback and massaged his knee. I was in the other chair and Dan was in my marriage counselor's seat, facing the two of us.

"Let's have what you've got on Gracie Brill." He started writing before I even began speaking.

"During our appointment, Gracie showed no signs that would indicate suicidal intentions. She acted as if, well as if she had a new lease on life. Sometimes suicide attempts will do that to a person. They seem to come back from the experience ready to live more fully than they ever have before."

"But didn't you see her right before her last attempt?"

"Yes."

"Well, did you know she was suicidal then?"

"No," I said. "Sometimes there are no detectable signs."

"Then why couldn't she have done it again?"

"Because when I look back over the session we had before the first time, I could see that the content — that is, early childhood memories — could have torn her apart and made her more likely to do something drastic under stress. Plus, the man she loved had just told her that he would be leaving his wife so he could be with Gracie."

"I don't get it. Why wouldn't that news make her happy?"

"Because she never really wanted to have a normal unencumbered relationship with him. She's too scared of that kind of intimacy. That's why she picked a married man."

He continued to write.

"And when I look back at this last session, I see healthy responses to her problems. She's resolving problems, not just unearthing bleak memories. Plus, I have to tell you my biggest reason for suspecting foul play."

He was writing furiously now.

"You see, the man she loved is seriously disturbed."

"Name?"

"Eliot Wohlman."

"Why didn't you tell me this before?"

"I did tell you about Eliot. I just didn't tell you he was involved with Gracie."

He sighed. "So he had been visiting Gracie when he came after you in the parking lot?"

"Yes. My next contact with him was here, in the office. He came under the pretext of wanting to apologize for his behavior in the parking lot. But it was an act. I know it was. He wanted me to think of him as a good man, but troubled."

"You're sure that's wrong?" the detective asked.

"It was too radical, unbelievable. That man was dangerous in the parking lot. I think he tried to kill Gracie this time."

He shook his head. "Pretty iffy stuff."

"For what it's worth," Dan said, "Sophie is usually on target."

"I'm sure she is but as I said, everything we have is a supposition." He turned to me. "Why would he want her dead?"

"Many reasons," I said. "She broke up with him in the hospital. If she ever told any of his colleagues they were an item, he'd be off their referral list to say the least. And she could tell his wife too."

Samms sat back in his chair. "So suddenly he's got second thoughts about this relationship with Gracie and tries to kill her?"

"She was the one with second thoughts. And he's threatened by that. He's threatened by me too, because of all the information I have about him. He knows I intend to have his license revoked. He's got three reasons to kill her. One is to get me sued and thrown off the hospital staff. Two is to stop her from betraying him publicly, and three, which is the most primitive, or most basic, is because he can deal with her death easier than her dismissal of him. And that's why he gave Jeanne, that other patient I told you about, the Dalmane."

The three of us looked out the window at the sun reflecting off the water. The captain was standing on the bow of the *Pilgrim*. His husky was next to him. I saw the captain bend over. The dog licked his face. It looked like they were both laughing.

"You say she's still in a coma?" Samms said.

"Yes."

"I'd like to take a look at her anyway."

"What is there to see?" Dan asked.

"I have no idea," the detective said.

A half hour later, Samms and I were standing next to Gracie's bed. There had been no change in her status.

He gently turned down the bed sheet. Without touching her, he looked at her feet and legs. Then he bent over her and looked at her neck and head. He looked at the stitches on her wrist, being careful not to get in the way of the IV.

He looked closely at her right wrist for a long time. Then he went to the other side of the bed and peered at her left wrist.

"What is it?" I asked.

He didn't look at me. "I'll tell you in a minute," he said. For another painstaking few moments, he repeated the process of examining both wrists. Finally, he motioned for me to look.

"See these lines?"

"No."

"Bend down and look real close over here." He pointed to an area slightly below the stitches. There were tiny faint lines all around her wrist as if she had been wearing a too-tight bracelet.

"What do you think would do that?" he asked.

"I don't know. Why don't you just tell me?" He ignored my insolence.

"A rope would do that, a very small but strong rope. Clever," he mused almost to himself. "Somebody was smart enough to know that these marks would just about be camouflaged into the stitches."

"Well, what do we do now?" I asked.

"Any idea how long she'll be out?"

"I'm afraid not," I said.

"Where's her car?"

"Doctor Corbut said it was towed to the police station."

He rubbed the back of his neck. "I'll go take a look at that. If I have anything to tell you, I'll phone." He started to leave the room.

"Wait a minute," I called. "Let's go together. I don't want to walk out alone."

Along the corridor, hospital personnel went about their tasks, not paying much attention to us. At least I wasn't the subject of hospital gossip yet.

"How are you holding up under all this?" Samms asked.

"Sometimes okay, sometimes not. It doesn't seem very real at times. I realize my job can be dangerous. I've just never seen it come at me like this."

We were in the parking lot. One row of cars away from us, I saw Eliot Wohlman walking toward the front door.

"There's Eliot," I whispered, my pulse speeding.

"Let's go have a little chat." He began walking in Eliot's direction.

"Just like that?" I asked. "You're going to go right up to him?"

He walked briskly with me trailing along side of him. "In my business, you just don't let the alleged perpetrator trot right by you. Doctor Wohlman?" he called.

Eliot stopped and quickly looked behind him. Probably measuring the distance between himself and his car. I was as scared as he looked. But he stood his ground as we approached.

"Are you here to visit Gracie Brill?"

"How did you know that?" Eliot asked.

"I understand that you're a friend of hers."

Eliot made no comment.

"Frankly, Wohlman," Samms said, "I'm not entirely satisfied that Ms. Brill was alone when she was injured."

"I don't have to talk to you at all. I can simply refuse until I speak to a lawyer."

"That's right. You can do that."

"I wasn't with her when she did it, I'll tell you that." He looked at me with his chilling dark eyes and started to walk away.

"How did you know she was in the hospital?" Samms called after him.

"I left several messages on her answering machine and was concerned when she didn't return my calls. I'm sure Doctor Green told you about her other suicide attempt."

Samms nodded.

"I was worried this morning and went to her house. Her car wasn't there and I waited outside. It was too early for her to be going anywhere. When I returned home, I decided that there was a chance that she'd be back in the hospital, knowing how fragile a girl she is."

That was smart of him. Leaving messages on her machine added credibility to his story.

"Did you see or speak to anyone between the hours of..." he looked at his notes, "four PM and seven AM?"

Eliot pretended to think this over.

"No, I didn't," he said.

"What about your wife?" I asked.

"She's out of town."

"Isn't that convenient," I said. Samms gave me a look.

"So no one can attest to the fact that you were not with Gracie Brill during that time?" Samms said.

"What are you getting at? Gracie is an unstable girl. It doesn't surprise me that she tried to kill herself again."

"How did you know that?" Samms asked.

"Know what?"

"That she tried to kill herself."

"Because you said that."

"No, I said that I questioned whether she was alone when she was injured."

Wohlman looked around nervously. "Well, probably when I called the hospital to see if she had been admitted, someone must have told me what happened."

"No one would give out that kind of information. Isn't that correct, Doctor Green?"

"That's right," I said.

"They'd give it to me. I'm a doctor," he said.

"Not with a psych admission," I said. "Not unless you were directly involved with her treatment."

I could tell by the muscles around Eliot's jaw that he was clenching his teeth. "Then I must have just assumed it. Why else would she be back in the hospital so soon?"

He stared at me like he was daring me to draw first. I didn't move.

"All right, Wohlman," Samms said. "That's all for now, but we might have some further questions later on."

"I suppose you're going to tell me not to take any trips, right?" he said with a feeble smile.

"That's right. Don't do that."

As Samms walked me to the Blazer, I said, "Now, do you know what I mean?"

"Everything he said could be true."

"Oh, come on," I said. "He was scared."

"Most people are when they're talking to me." I saw that his leg was giving him a hard time. His limp was getting pretty bad.

"So you don't think he's dangerous?" I said.

"I didn't say that." We waved to Dan, who looked relieved to see us approaching.

"We try to make decisions based on what we know, rather than allusions. Thank God you're not a detective."

Dan got out of the car to greet us.

"Thank God you're not a shrink," I called after him, as he limped to his car.

When we arrived home, I checked in with my service to find there were no messages. I brewed a pot of coffee. I put two tablespoons of cocoa in a mug and poured the coffee over it. I said to Dan, who was going through the mail, "I'm going to take a bath. Visitors are welcome."

"Mom," Robin called out from the kitchen. "Don't stay in the tub too long. I'm making a surprise for dinner."

"Okay, Robin."

To Dan I whispered, "The last thing I feel like doing is eating."

"I don't think I've ever heard you say that. Do the best you can. She feels sorry for you and wants to cheer you up."

"What's she making?"

"She wouldn't say."

I went upstairs and nixed the bath. Perhaps my favorite nightshirt would comfort me instead. It was seven years old, with red stripes and holes. The mocha and the rocker by the window sounded good, too.

There was a knock on the door.

"Mom?"

"Come in, sweets. I'm just sitting."

She came in and sat on the bed. She had on a Syracuse University sweatshirt and jeans, and fluffy pink slippers. She was wearing the pink seed pearl bracelet I had given her.

"What are you cooking?" I asked.

"It's a surprise."

"I hate surprises."

"I know."

It was great having her here voluntarily. She went over to my bureau and started looking through the jewelry box.

"So, how's it going?" She pulled out a pair of white scallop shell earrings.

"I could use a vacation."

She held the earrings to her ears and looked in the mirror above the bureau, turning her head from side to side. I sipped the hot liquid and watched her.

"I, um." She picked up a strand of pearls and held them across her forehead. "I'm sorry that things aren't going well."

My little girl.

"It'll pass soon, sweetie. Most of the time, it's not like this."

"Do you ever think of quitting your job?"

"Nope. I like it, most of the time."

"Do you think that Dad would be happier if you quit?"

"He'd have less to worry about," I said. "But I don't think he'd be happier. Do you worry about me?" I took a soothing sip.

"Of course I do."

"Lately I can't say I blame you."

"Did you used to worry about things a lot when you were my age?" she asked.

"Constantly. But most of the things I worried about never happened, so I learned that worrying didn't make much sense unless there was something I could do about it." Who was I kidding?

"Who are you kidding, Mom?"

We both laughed.

"So tell me," I said. "What's so appealing about Colorado or California? Does wanting to go have anything to do with not having too many friends here?" I hated that she thought about going to the opposite end of the country.

"I don't know." She shrugged her shoulders. "I guess I just want to get away from here. All the kids who just want to get married and stay on the Cape seem to be so narrow. I don't know. I want my own life somewhere away from here, Mom."

"Well that's certainly a natural way to feel." Oh how I wished it wasn't.

She turned to leave and said, "Dinner will be ready in about ten minutes."

"What is it?"

"It's a surprise."

When I arrived in the kitchen, wonderful aromas were wafting through the room. Dan and Robin were busily setting the table. They instructed me to sit.

"What's cooking?" I asked.

"Wait and see," Dan said.

Though I had no hunger, I would do my best for my daughter.

Robin grabbed two potholders and brought out a beautiful meatloaf with four slices of bacon on top.

"Oh, my heart!" I said.

She put it in the center of the table. From the microwave, Dan brought a steaming bowl of mashed potatoes. Before he put it down, Robin sprinkled on some chives. On the range was a boiling saucepan of string beans. Robin drained the beans, then added butter and almonds.

"Oh, Robin," I said. "This is my favorite meal."

"You say that about everything." She sliced the meatloaf, putting two of the pieces of bacon on mine. She insisted on serving us and carefully arranged each plate, making sure that we each had some chives on our potatoes.

"Oh Robin," I said between meatloaf bites, "you did great."

"Thanks."

We ate in silence. I wished I had felt more lively, especially since Robin had gone to such trouble. At least I could see that she was eating a decent amount of food for a change. That made me feel better.

"It's okay, Sophie," Dan said, reading my mind and touching my arm. "Robin just wanted to make something special while things are going crazy for all of us. You don't need to be your effervescent self. Just relax and enjoy your meal."

"You two are priceless," I said. "And everything's delicious. Thank you, Robin. Words cannot say how much I appreciate this."

"You're welcome," she said and began to say something else, but stopped herself.

"What?" I asked.

"Oh, nothing," she said and continued to eat.

"If something's wrong, I can handle it," I said. Dan looked worried.

"It's nothing like that."

"Well, what is it?" I asked.

"I have some good news I wanted to tell you and Dad about together, but I don't want you to make a big deal out of it."

"Robin." I pointed my fork at her face. "If you don't tell me right now, I'm going to stick this fork in your eye."

"Okay, okay." She giggled. "I've sort of got a job."

"That's great, honey!" Dan said.

"What kind of a job?" The fork was still in position.

"It's not a real job, I mean I don't get paid or anything."

"Robin," I said.

"I'm tutoring three girls in French."

"You are?" I said.

"Doctor Freedman, you know, the school psychologist, thought it might be a good way for me to channel my creative energy, since I'm good at French anyway."

Dan shot me a warning glance.

"Well, Doctor Freedman sounds like she's got a good head on her shoulders," I said. Both of them were waiting for some wisecrack from me.

"Tell us all about it," Dan said.

"Well, there are three girls. You don't know them; Sonja Tibbits, Carol Hingham and Debbie Nickerson, and they need help in French."

"When do you see them?" I asked.

"During lunch hour."

"You don't eat?"

"Yes, Mother. We all eat together while we're doing our French," she said. "I really like it."

"I think it's fantastic," I said. "I'm all for it and I'm really fine about the counselor thing."

"Good for you," Dan said with a patronizing pat on my back. "That's just as big an accomplishment as Robin's."

"Channeling her creative energy," I muttered under my breath.

"What?" he said.

"Nothing."

Chapter Seventeen

Wednesday, 7 AM

The morning was cold. The skies emitted a combination of sleet and snow showers. I put on my gray wool skirt and blazer. I attached my great grandmother's stick pin to my lapel. It was a small sea horse made of emeralds. The eye was a ruby.

"I haven't seen you wear that pin in years," Dan said.

"I haven't, and I have no idea what possessed me to wear it today."

"Maybe you want her spirit around you."

"I could use all the help I can get."

I drank coffee on the couch while waiting for Robin's ride to pick her up and take her to school. A car slowed and honked. Robin came running from the kitchen with an Oreo in her mouth and grabbed her books and purse.

"Bye," she called as she ran out the front door.

Dan and I put on our coats and left, after locking the door and setting the alarm.

The driving was slippery and uncomfortable. In the short time it took us to get from the parking lot to my building, we were wet and chilled.

"Dan," I said, "you can't just sit in the waiting room all day."

"Oh, yes I can."

"Please, honey, I can handle this."

"I don't know…"

"Please. Go."

"Well…I'll be back when you're through and we'll go to the hospital." He hesitated. "I really hate to leave you alone."

"Go, go. I'll call you if I need to talk."

The three people I was seeing this morning were the patients I transferred from yesterday. My first one was a twenty-eight-year-old heir to over five million dollars and about as chronically depressed as anyone could get. Second was a twenty-one-year-old bulimic girl, who lived with her father in spite of a strong desire to move away. She couldn't, as she said, abandon her dad.

Third on the agenda was a sixty-two-year-old woman who was over-involved with her two daughters' lives. She spent the session talking about how she couldn't stand her younger daughter's husband.

For lunch, I searched through the fridge and found peanut butter that I spread on saltines.

After two more patients, I was through for the day. I found Dan in the waiting room. He looked awful, like he had aged ten years.

"You don't look good," I said.

"I know. And you must be bushed," he said.

"I am. People think this is a cushy job. It's not easy concentrating hard for so long."

"It's like taking six classes in a row," he said.

"No, it's more like teaching six classes in a row."

It was still sleeting when we drove to the hospital.

I picked up Gracie's chart, saw that there were no changes, and headed to her room. I looked down at her, lying in bed. Her lovely gray hair was spread out on the pillow.

She shouldn't be lying in a hospital with a goddamned IV and an oxygen mask. I was so angry at everything. I was just so damn angry!

"Please, Gracie. Please come out of this."

No response.

I decided to keep talking out loud anyhow. After looking around to make sure no one was standing near the doorway, I said, "Oh Gracie, you are such a beautiful girl...so young. There are many years lying ahead that belong to you." I felt an ache in my throat from holding back tears. "Why do you take this short space of time that we have on earth and make such foolish choices?"

I was saying all the things I felt like saying in therapy, but believed I couldn't.

"All the men you pick are so bad for you. It's so obvious, Gracie. Why can't you just see that?"

I slammed her chart down on the foot of the bed and went to the window. There was an old couple walking slowly toward the hospital, holding hands. What was the story behind their visit? Probably seeing a daughter, although I had no idea why I thought that. Appendicitis? Fibroid tumors? We automatically make up scenarios, the majority of which are way off the mark.

I could have sworn I heard a sound behind me.

I turned around quickly, but saw no one at the door. Gracie was lying still. Turning back, I saw the couple as they were about to enter the hospital. They were laughing.

Another sound. A swishing noise.

I went over to Gracie's bed.

"Gracie," I said. "I keep hearing noises. Is it you?"

Nothing.

I brushed some hair off her forehead and watched her peaceful face. I prayed that I'd never have to see my daughter in this cold fugue.

"Gracie," I said, "I've got to go now. I'll see you tomorrow." I picked up her chart from the bed and headed toward the door.

That noise again.

Swish. Swish.

Her left arm moved back and forth on the sheet and stopped.

"Gracie!" I ran to her. "Gracie!"

Her eyes were closed but her facial muscles were moving. I removed the mask.

"I'm here, Gracie. It's Doctor Green."

I picked up her left hand and rubbed it softly between both of mine. There was a barely perceptible nod.

"Don't go away, Gracie. I'm here."

A sound came from her throat, a word I couldn't understand.

"Gracie." I continued to caress her hand. "Please, dear. Talk to me. Come on, Gracie. Come on now."

Her eyes were still closed, but her lips parted again. "Doctor…"

"Yes, it's me. Doctor Green. I'm here, Gracie. Go ahead."

Silence.

Nothing.

"Please, Gracie. Wake up now. I'm here to listen to you."

Her lips parted again, and her eyes opened like little slits, although she wasn't focusing.

"Did you try to kill yourself?" I whispered close to her ear. She didn't respond.

"Gracie, can you answer me? Did you try to kill yourself?"

She uttered, "N-n-no," and attempted to shake her head. The effort to move her head seemed to exhaust her and her eyes closed again.

"Gracie," I urged, "please talk to me."

I waited for an eternity.

No response.

After a few more minutes of coaxing, it became clear that she could say no more. I replaced the mask.

"It's good that you spoke to me," I said. "I'll be here tomorrow. But it's such a good sign that you woke up, even though you got tired again." I touched her cheek. "You're going to be fine. That's the best part."

I lovingly stroked her forehead. "You're going to be just fine."

I went to the nurses' station and entered my notes into her chart. I was told that Phil Corbut would be coming on duty in about two hours and would be informed of the changes. Two nurses rushed into Gracie's room after hearing about her episode.

I called Detective Samms from the hospital and told him what happened. He had wanted me to keep him posted on Gracie's condition and I didn't think it would be a problem if I did.

Outside the hospital, I found Dan sitting in the Blazer and told him the news.

"Let's go home," I said. "I'm so tired."

"I have to run to the center for ten minutes. The social worker lost her keys and I have to go lock up. I want you to come with me."

"Oh I just can't Dan. You won't be long, and I'm dying to get home. We've got the burglar alarm. I don't have the energy to argue. Just go, and come back soon. It would make me feel better if you went."

"Well..."

"I'm beat. Just drop me off. That alarm's connected to the police. Just don't take too long. And while you're out, could you pick something up for supper?"

"I don't want to take any more time away from you than I have to. I'll come home as soon as I can and I'll make us supper."

"Great," I said.

"You must be a wreck if you don't want to know what I'm going to make."

"I do want to know," I said.

"How about a big tuna salad platter with onions, lettuce and tomatoes?"

"No potato salad?"

"Too fattening."

I let it pass.

At the house, he waited in the truck for me to get inside safely. I turned off the alarm with my key and went inside.

"Everything's fine," I yelled out the front door. "Hurry back."

"Put the alarm back on from the inside," I heard him say. I did as he asked and waved from the window.

"Robin?" I called. There was what she termed "music" coming from her room. She couldn't hear me.

I kicked off my flats and plopped on the couch. I was too tired to change out of my work clothes. A tuna dinner would not cut the mustard. I'd have to carbo load before Dan came back.

There was a quick knocking sound in the kitchen.

My heart skipped a beat. Lately, every little tap sent me into a panic.

I found the remote control under a cushion on the couch and put on the tube. God forbid I ever get up and do it manually.

The airways were cluttered with talk shows. I usually placed their content on par with *People Magazine* and therefore loved them. At present was a panel of six people of varying sizes and shapes. They were all previously employed as exhibitionists in a circus. The prevailing topic was the question of exploitation and whether these people had choices. I wasn't sure.

The phone rang.

"Hello?"

"It's Samms." He sounded agitated.

"What's the matter?"

"I'm at the hospital. Gracie woke up again."

"I'll be there as soon as I can."

"No need. She's tired, but fine. You intuition was right about her not trying to kill herself this time."

"I told you that! What happened?"

"She didn't stay awake long enough to say. Don't answer your door to anyone."

"But I'm scared! Dan's not home!"

"I'll have one of my men in your neighborhood right away. Put your alarm on."

"I did."

"And don't answer the door. Not even a 'who's there?'"

"Okay."

He hung up.

Another knock from the kitchen.

I stiffened.

Sophie, go check it out.

No, I said to myself. You're uptight because of the phone call. If there was a murderer in your kitchen, he wouldn't be sitting in there for the last fifteen minutes perusing your refrigerator.

Knock. Screech. The sound of metal on metal.

I couldn't move.

Go ahead, Sophie. Get the hell over there and check out the kitchen. Go!

I walked quietly to the kitchen. Slowly, I pushed open the door. The sight in front of me made my head nearly explode.

Robin was in a chair. Her mouth was gagged and her face was horror stricken. Behind her stood Eliot Wohlman, aiming a gun at my daughter's temple.

"Good evening, Sophie."

Robin's eyes pleaded with me for help. Her cheeks were soaked with tears and blood.

"Don't move," he said to Robin. "Your mother's had a tough day and we wouldn't want to worry her now, would we?"

"How did you get past the alarm?"

"Your daughter invited me in. She's very polite."

I stared at my Robin. My body systems were operating at breakneck speeds, in flight-or-fight human reflex.

"What do you want, Eliot?"

"How kind of you to be concerned about what I want," he said. "And I didn't even think you liked me anymore."

Robin began to squirm. Her hands were tied behind her. Eliot pushed the gun into Robin's temple. She winced with pain.

Oh, my daughter. My girl. Please God. It's my little girl!

I saw the pink seed pearl bracelet broken, the beads scattered on the floor behind her.

"The papers came today," he said, standing there motionless. Only his eyes and his gun holding hand showed any movement. "You've ruined me."

He jammed the gun into Robin's head. A drop of blood ran down her face. I could see her shaking.

"What papers, Eliot?"

"What papers?" he said, with an incredulous expression. "You're going to fuck around with me now?"

"I don't know what you're talking about!"

"Right. Of course you don't." He paused, thinking for a moment. "It would have been better if Gracie had died. Although Henry Broussard would have had a stroke if she did. He and I are old pals. I had to tell him about you, warn him about your incompetence. But there's something I want to know."

"What is it, Eliot?"

"How did you know?"

"Know what?"

"You're pushing your luck, Doctor. And your daughter's going to feel it."

"I do not know what you are asking me!" I was jumping out of my skin with terror.

"My California license. You knew it was revoked fifteen years ago for screwing two patients."

"I don't know anything about that!"

He laughed. "How can you lie when your daughter's in such a state?"

I couldn't figure out what to do next. "I just got a call from Detective Samms," I said. "Gracie is conscious. She'll tell the truth about you."

"I know she will. It was just a matter of time."

I prayed that the cop Samms was sending over would be here soon. What was taking him so long?

"If you get out now, you'll have time to get away," I said.

"Bullshit. You know I'll never get away with this. They'll find out I tried to kill Gracie. I botched it. I forced her in the car with my gun. I tied her hands to the steering wheel until she passed out. Then I removed the ropes. But that was my big mistake. By opening the door, I must have let in enough oxygen to save her life. How could you make me do this to such a good girl?"

"Tell me what you want, Eliot." I spoke slowly, not moving, not taking my eyes off of him. He was going out of the realm of reality. I could tell by the vacancy in his eyes.

"It's been so gratifying terrorizing you all along."

I didn't move.

He slowly reached behind him on the counter and pulled up my car phone. "Here you go, Sophie. I wouldn't want to be accused of stealing."

He started laughing, and it escalated to a non-human sounding haunted house roar. The gun abraded Robin's skin with the tempo of his laughter. More blood dripped. She looked up at me so pathetically. My heart was shattering into a million pieces.

"I should have made your brakes fail," he said.

"So you sent that note with the roses?"

"Of course I did. I knew you'd think it was Carl, him being a mechanic."

"How did you know about that?"

He slowly shook his head from side to side. "Now you're making me very annoyed at you. If I've told you once, I've told you a hundred times I've known about Carl through my police connections for years. Don't you ever listen?" He rolled his eyes. "And you call yourself a psychiatrist."

"I...love you...Robin," I said in a whisper. "We're going to get out of this."

Eliot glared at me. His face contained a thousand years of fury.

"You think you're getting out of this?" he shouted. "My life is a piece of shit." His mouth contorted. There were tears forming in his eyes. It was then I felt the stab of terror because his last semblance of sanity was gone.

I couldn't think of my next move. I frantically tried to think clearly, to decide what to do.

"Eliot," I said, inching slowly toward Robin, "I'm just going to sit next to my daughter, so she won't be so scared."

"Forget it!" he snapped.

Robin's head was trembling. He pinched her cheek, hard. "Keep up the shaking and you'll be dead."

The trembling stopped and her face turned ghostly white. Robin was going into shock. Her eyes were glazed and unfocused.

Eliot waved the gun at the chair next to Robin. "Have a seat. We can't have your daughter upset."

Thank God.

I started to go to the chair. In a flash, he fired a shot into the floor, a few inches in front of my foot.

"Just kidding, Sophie," he said. "What do you think I am, crazy or something?" The laughter rose to a high pitch. "I had to come here. You can't destroy my life and just walk away. I ask you — where would the justice be in that?"

If I could get him to open the back door, the alarm would sound.

"You were right to do what you did," I said. "You didn't have any other choice. There's the door, Eliot. You still have time."

"Spare me the reverse psychology crap. It doesn't look good on your daughter's face." He twisted the gun into her skin. The end of it was bloody.

What would buy me time until the cop came? He was too smart for any more ploys. I had to keep him talking.

"Okay, Eliot. I'll stop the psychology crap and I'll stop trying to manipulate you, since I can't figure out how to do it."

He glowered with self-satisfaction. He then looked at his watch. "Where's your husband? I expected him to be here."

"At his center," I said.

"What's he doing there at this time of night?"

"Locking it up."

"I don't believe you," he said.

"Call the center. He's probably there now."

The phone rang. We all jumped.

After three rings, the answering machine kicked in. "Hello, you have reached the Green family…" Dan's voice recording said.

Let it be Dan. Please, God.

He knows I often don't answer the phone in the evenings, and that I screen the calls, but he'd panic if I didn't pick it up while he was leaving a message.

"We're unable to take your call right now…" The message went on interminably.

"At the sound of the tone…" Sweat was forming on my forehead.

"Please leave your name, your number, and a message…"

Eliot growled, "Pick it up if it's him."

"And we'll return your call as soon as possible."

Then came the beep.

"It's me," I heard Dan say.

"Pick it up or she won't have a face." He pushed the gun in further where Robin's skin was scraped and bleeding. My daughter looked catatonic.

"Where are you?" I heard Dan ask.

Eliot cocked the hammer of the gun.

"Okay!" I said, and picked up the phone.

"Hello, Dan."

The machine stopped recording because I had picked up. Eliot couldn't hear Dan's part of the conversation.

"What's wrong?" he asked.

"Nothing's wrong. Really."

"I know it is. Oh Christ," he said. "Now listen carefully. If you say, 'I swear that nothing's wrong,' I'll call the police."

I took a deep breath and looked over at Eliot holding my daughter's life in his hands, and said, "I swear that nothing's wrong, but thanks for checking in on me. We're hunky dory and starving to death."

Dan said, "I love you, Sophie," and hung up.

"I love you too," I said to the empty line, and felt a lump in my throat as I slowly placed the phone back on the hook.

Keep talking Eliot, I said to myself. Just keep it up a little while longer. I didn't move.

"You told my wife about Jeanne and Gracie," he said.

"I didn't!"

"Oh you did." He reached in his back pocket and pulled out some papers. "She filed for divorce."

"Eliot, I—"

"Oh please. Don't start with me. You know all about it. How do you think the grounds of cruel and inhuman treatment look on my record?"

"I don't know anything about this!"

"Sure you don't. Nancy said I 'publicly flaunted my relationships with other women' and there was 'constant screaming and verbal abuse.' Where do you think she learned those words? From the paperboy? She wasn't happy with just adultery. She had to file for cruel and inhuman treatment. Very nice touch, Sophie. And bringing in the licensing board in California cinched the deal."

"Eliot, a lawyer would find out about your licensing history. And a lawyer would be the one to use those legal divorce terms. Not me."

"Really? Would a lawyer have told her about the others, too?"

"What?"

"You're such an actress. The only way Nancy would have known about all the others was by hearing it from her very best friend, Cape Cod's most prominent psychiatrist, Doctor Sophie Green. I know you both meet for lunch every week. I know all about your conspiring."

"I swear I don't know what you're talking about. I've never discussed anything with Nancy. I don't even know about any women other than Jeanne and Gracie."

"Oh my lovely impressionable Gracie. You forced her to end it with me. I needed her. You've destroyed everything I have — my marriage, my career, my relationships with the women I loved. You took away everything…" His voice sounded distant. "And now…" he centered the gun on the back of Robin's head, "I'm taking something away from you."

Just then, Robin shoved her chair backwards into Eliot's torso and I made my move. In an instant, I dove for his ankles, knocking his feet out from under him so that he fell hard on top of me. I grabbed his wrist with both hands and dug my fingernails into his flesh.

"Drop it, Eliot! Give me the damn gun!"

Our faces were only inches apart as we lay sprawled on the floor. He struggled and looked fiercely at me with rage in his eyes.

"Never hurt a child in front of her mother," I grunted through clenched teeth. I squeezed his wrist harder. He tried to pry me off with his other hand. With everything I had in me, I kneed him in the groin. The jolt made him drop the gun. Still lying on the floor, I stretched out toward it, but now he had his hands around my throat.

"Sophie, you lose."

I couldn't stop him from strangling me. Out of the corner of my eye, I saw Robin try to move her chair toward the gun. An animal sound escaped from my throat as I tried to stop her.

Horrified, I watched as she snaked out of the rope that was tying her hands. She wrenched off the gag from her mouth and fell to the floor on top of the gun.

I was losing consciousness.

Eliot let go of me when he saw her kneeling on the floor, holding the gun in both quivering hands.

"I'm going to shoot this," she said. The gun was aimed at Eliot. He didn't move.

"Don't Robin," I choked out.

The gun was swaying. Eliot stayed where he was.

"Give it to me, sweetheart." I crawled to her, but she held the gun, still on her knees, facing Eliot.

I managed to get behind her, and put both arms slowly around my daughter. I firmly gripped the gun.

"I've got it, Robin. We're safe."

She let go and sank to the floor.

Eliot laughed.

At that instant, an explosive noise filled the room. The burglar alarm siren wailed at deafening levels. Two officers, yelling the word "Police!" crashed through the front and back doors with their pistols pointed.

One shouted, "Put down the gun!"

I put it on the floor.

The other cop said, "That's Doctor Green." I recognized him from the parking lot.

Feeling woozy, I reached for Robin.

"Sweetheart, sweetheart," I covered her face with kisses. She sat on the floor with me as we hugged and cried and swayed.

"I thought you were out of it," I said, cradling her head in my arms.

"Mom," she whispered. She was pale and shaking.

In the distance, I could hear the officer reciting Eliot's rights to him. He was already handcuffed.

"Robin," I cooed to my daughter, "I love you."

I could barely hear her say, "I love you too, Mom."

Over her shoulder Dan appeared. He didn't say a word, just got down on the floor with us in a three-way embrace. He kissed Robin and then he gave me a kiss like there was no tomorrow.

Before being led out to the patrol car, Eliot turned to me and said, "It's not over." I held my daughter protectively and didn't answer.

One of the policemen said, "We radioed Detective Samms on our way here, Mrs. Green, so we'll let him do most of the questioning, but I do need to ask you a few things right now, if you feel you can handle it."

"It's Doctor Green," Robin mumbled, her eyes half shut. "My mother's a doctor."

"Oh, sorry, Doctor Green," he said. "No offense."

"None taken," I whispered.

I answered the routine questions while I sat on the floor. Dan went into the bathroom and came back with some cotton balls and Bactine.

"I'll do it," I said, and tenderly patted away the blood on my daughter's temple.

Samms came fifteen minutes later and asked for a detailed description of the events. Dan paled as he heard me answer his questions. Samms stayed for coffee. Dan and I had a glass of sherry. Robin had most of mine. When Samms left, Robin went upstairs. I picked up the seed pearls from the floor and put them in a plastic bag to be restrung. Then I went up to see her. She was in the bathroom, but had left the door open. She was looking in the mirror, and still not focusing. I watched her touch her reflection. She turned on the faucet and wet her finger and slowly outlined her face. Then she saw my face in the mirror. I didn't say a word. I stood next to her and wet my finger and outlined her face and then outlined mine.

"We're both here, my love," I said.

She turned her head and looked at me, but didn't speak. I cradled her chin in both of my hands. "I have something to say to you, my daughter." And finally her eyes focused on mine and we looked at each other in a moment of connection I would never forget. "You are my hero."

Chapter Eighteen

Thursday, 7 AM

I woke needing a few minutes to make absolutely sure it all wasn't a dream and that our torture had truly come to an end. Dan was up already. At noon, we were to have a lobster extravaganza with Mark and Rosie, my parents, and special guests of honor, Detective Samms and his wife.

From bed, I called my mother and apologized for all the worry.

She said, "If you didn't want me to worry, then you shouldn't work in that meshugeneh job of yours."

"But you and Dad are the ones who paid for medical school."

"I thought you'd meet a doctor there."

"Say, Ma," I said. "How about we spend the day together the next time we're both free for a whole day? We could go to Boston and see what's showing at the Fine Arts Museum and maybe walk around the North End?"

"I think your father would feel left out."

"Trust me, Ma. He won't."

"That sounds like too long a day for me," she said.

I almost let it go, but I've learned that I was losing too many moments to time, a commodity that would not go on endlessly. I was not going to let more connections go out of my reach forever.

"We'll just go to the museum then. It will be a wonderful day."

"All right, Sophie. We'll stop at Filene's Basement as long as we're there."

We were about to hang up. "Let's decide on a date right now, Ma. You pick the day."

She thought for a moment. "I'm free next Tuesday."

I had a full day of patients that day. "Next Tuesday's perfect," I said.

"It's a date, then."

I lazed in bed for a while, thinking about all that had happened and all the people involved.

I only wished that Carl Darby had been found. But life is never tied up in neat packages. Poor Elizabeth. I will never forget her. I can't say that she made anybody's life any better but mine. She helped to free me from the grip of my past.

And Charlie Downey. I hoped he would respond to my request to see him once more. It was certainly easier for him to blame me for his mother's death than to blame himself. But I was determined to do the right thing and help him see through this defense. For my sake and for his.

There is a special place in my heart for Gracie. Thank God she's okay. Phil Corbut expects her out of the hospital in two or three days. What she must have gone through. It's been increasingly harder to maintain my objectivity with her. Who am I to tell anyone else how to live their life?

Of course, my daughter is exempt from my newfound humbleness.

Robin. What does she say to her counselor? How will she adjust to the horror she was a part of? Maybe it's good that she's seeing a professional. I hope this woman knows what she's doing. I'd give up my perfect nose if I could read her files.

My wonderful Dan. He wanted so much to save me — to make everything better. I kid him about his male oriented attitude, but he has taught me that this kind of love has nothing to do with gender. Of course I should know that. I'd give up anything, even my life, for him or Robin — if that would save them from disaster.

How did I ever get so lucky having Dan as a husband? Over the years, people have told me he's "too good to be true" and everyone who's said that has been right.

By eleven o'clock, I was dressed in my clambake finest, a pair of oversized jeans sans knees and one of Dan's work shirts. Robin came into the kitchen wearing her pink running outfit. "That's gonna be all greasy and smelly in about four hours," I said.

"Not everybody eats like Henry the Eighth, Mom."

Wallace Samms and his wife, Norma, arrived at quarter to noon. They had taken me up on my suggestion to wear something extra casual and possibly dispensable. He had on old brown pants and a UCLA sweatshirt, but naturally he came in wearing his awful herringbone coat. Norma was wearing a gray smock. I greeted her warmly. "You can't imagine what your husband has had to put up with around here," I said.

"I'm so happy that you're all right," she said. "And please excuse the way we're dressed. Wallace insisted we come like this."

"That's exactly what I told him," I said, and led them into the kitchen. "With this kind of meal, expect to get down and dirty."

Robin rolled her eyes. How quickly they turn back into little snotfaces. She had her hair combed artfully over the bandage on her temple, with a brown barrette to keep it in place.

Mark and Rosie were next to arrive. Mark gave me a big emotional hug.

"I'm all right," I said.

"Oh, the trauma you've been through." His hug lingered on.

I tapped his back. "Really. It's okay now."

He continued to hug me.

"Mark, please." I looked over his shoulder and saw that Rosie was carrying a small duffel bag and shaking her head. With my brother still in the hug mode, I said, "What does Rosie have?"

"From one minute to the next, we never know when we'll be gone." He finally let go.

"We're not gone, Mark. See?" I pointed to Robin, who did a little curtsey.

He got the duffel bag and placed it gingerly on top of the table.

"Mark," I said, "just tell us what's in the bag."

He carefully unzipped it while saying, "We need to have something that will last forever...something that will be there if you're..." He turned toward me. "Oh, Sophie!" He began to approach me with his arms outstretched.

"Back, Mark! Back! If you hug me again, I'll put metal in your microwave."

I smiled uncomfortably at Norma Samms.

He went back to the bag and put his hand inside. Then, ever so delicately and tenderly, he brought out...a video camera. "For posterity, Sophie."

"I don't want to be remembered with lobster in my teeth," I said.

Norma Samms looked down at her smock.

"Sorry," Rosie said. "I couldn't talk him out of it."

My mother and father entered the kitchen. We introduced them to the Samms.

"So you're the police detective," my mother said.

"Yes, ma'am."

"Call me Esther. Ma'am is for the store clerk. What does your mother say about what you do?"

"MO-THER!" I yelled.

"Just give me a chance to say hello here, Sophie. Do you have to put your nose into everybody's business? Don't you do enough of that at work?"

The big lobster pot was beginning to boil and I enlisted Dan's aid in plunging the nine crustaceans into the water. With him standing next to me at the stove, I had a perfect view of his left ear.

"It's gotten bigger," I said.

"What has?"

"That mole."

He stopped what he was doing. "If you bring up that mole again, I'm going to throw out all the peanut butter in the house, including the jar you think nobody knows about."

"The one in the bathroom? How did you know about that?"

"Ah ha! I didn't."

He was laughing as he finished putting the lobsters in the pot.

"You know they can feel that," Robin said.

"Robin," I said, "shellfish do not feel pain."

"Then why do they make noise when they're getting boiled to death?" she said.

"That's a myth," I said. "And you will discontinue this conversation if you want to live until tomorrow."

Mark picked up the camera.

The lobsters started knocking around in the pot.

Robin said, "I suppose they're just doing the cha-cha, Mom."

Mark pressed the record button and captured, for eternity, a shot of me looking at my daughter with a venomous sneer on my face. He panned the camera toward Robin, who smiled like a little angel.

Norma Samms had a funny look on her face.

"Can I help?" my father said. The others echoed his offer.

I gave everybody something to do. I steamed the clams and fried the sausages. I had real butter melting in a pan. Fries were in the microwave. When we brought the finished products to the table, I stood back and said, "It's all so wonderful, I could just die."

Mark picked up the camera and pressed RECORD.

"It's just an expression, Mark. Really. Dig in. Dig in everyone. This is a most happy occasion." I kissed Dan on the cheek and sat down. Everyone began reaching into bowls. Mark put the camera down after getting a wide shot of the eight of us with our plates overflowing.

Norma said, "I can't thank you enough for including us in your celebration, Doctor Green."

"Oh please, call me Sophie," I said. With a gloppy clam purposely hanging halfway out of my mouth, I garbled the words, "Tell me, do you honestly think I look like a doctor?"

Robin cracked up. My mother said, "Sophie, when you were a little girl, you used to think that dangling food out of your mouth was the funniest joke ever invented."

"Really?" I let the clam plop on my plate.

Robin was hysterical. Norma started giggling.

"Good fries, Mom," Robin said, and she dunked a whole handful in ketchup.

"I'll try a few of those babies," Mark said.

"You don't need salt," my mother said, and grabbed the shaker out of Samms' hand.

"What's this white thing in the sausage?" Robin asked.

We all cracked up. The combination of the celebration and the end of a long period of tension and fear made us let loose and feel great.

Samms said, "If I could get something to drink over here, I'd like to make a toast."

"Wonderful!" I said. "Diet Coke or beer?"

He wanted a beer. Among the nine of us, we shared six bottles of beer, which I insisted we put in wine glasses for the toast.

He stood up, raised his glass, and said, "Well, I for one, am glad it's all over."

"Amen," Dan said.

"I want to thank everyone in this fine family for a most delicious meal. You are an unusual group, to say the least."

We raised our glasses.

To me, he said, "I like you." I smiled at him and felt my eyes begin to water. "You are a special person, opinionated, stubborn and nuts at times." We all laughed. "I respect you. And...I want to tell you something else." He had tears in his eyes now too. "You'd make a crack detective." He turned to the rest. "So let's drink a toast to this great lady. If I may..." he said to me. "To Sophie."

"Thank you," I said, and let the tears flow. "That was lovely, really...thank you...Wallace."

And we drank.

The end